Country Blues

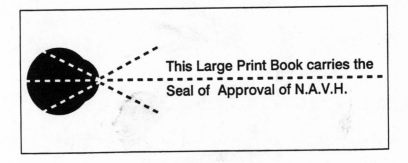

COUNTRY BLUES

Marjorie Everitt

Thorndike Press • Thorndike, Maine

Library of Congress Cataloging in Publication Data:

Everitt, Marjorie.
    Country blues / Marjorie Everitt.
        p.   cm.
    ISBN 1-56054-479-1 (alk. paper : lg. print)
    1. Large type books. I. Title.
[PS3555.V37C68   1992]   92-14920
813'.54—dc20   CIP

All the characters in this book are fictitious, and any resemblance to actual persons, living or dead, is purely coincidental.

Thorndike Press Large Print edition published in 1992 by arrangement with Avalon Books.

Cover photo by Thayer Smith.

The tree indicium is a trademark of Thorndike Press.

This book is printed on acid-free, high opacity paper. ∞

Country Blues

Prologue

The baby, a girl, was born on a quiet silver morning. A morning that was muffled by the ubiquitous San Francisco fog, wrapping itself around Coit Tower and the Ferry Building, burying the Bay Bridge, allowing only the tips of the graceful towers of the Golden Gate to taste the slanting rays of sunshine above the fog.

"What will you name her, then, missy?" the midwife asked in a quiet voice, watching the slim mother hold the tiny scrap of life as if she didn't quite know what it was. She wasn't built for childbearing, this one. The baby seemed healthy enough, though.

The young woman lying exhausted on the bed stirred slightly, staring toward the gray window of the small apartment. A little bird lit briefly on the sill and then, with a quick flutter of fragile wings, was gone.

"Wren?" the mother said. "Wrenbird, that's her name."

"Come into the kitchen," the third woman in the room said. A large and capable-looking woman, she took the midwife's arm and led her away from the birthing. Her mind was working surprisingly quickly, considering she'd had no sleep at all the night before.

"Put it down as Lauren Byrd," she told the midwife. "That's what she was trying to say." She knew better.

"The mother's name?" the midwife asked.

"Moonbeam." The larger woman spoke with resignation. And so it was that the baby's official, registered name became Lauren Byrd, child of Moonbeam Byrd, father unknown. . . .

The apartment in the Haight was small and crowded during the years of Lauren Byrd's childhood. The term flower child fit her mother perfectly, and so did the name Moonbeam. An early hippie, she floated through Lauren's memory with little more substance than a moonbeam or a dream.

It was big Auntie Nell who was more of a mother to her. Auntie Nell took in strays. Somewhere, there at the beginning, there had been an Uncle Joe, but he disappeared into the earliest of Lauren's memories.

Of her mother, she carried only two remembrances into her growing years: Moonbeam barefoot, in long skirts and beads, smiling over a storybook; Moonbeam in flowing multicolored caftan, looking like something from an Arthur Rackham drawing, as insubstantial as the blanketing fog.

Lauren was five when her mother died. She never knew why her mother died. "Because it was time," Auntie Nell told her gently. Later she was to wonder whether it was drugs, unstable health, or both. She never found out. Moonbeam was gone; Wrenbird lived on with Auntie Nell.

Quick and determined and bright, she did well in school. She was the last of Auntie Nell's strays, her "baby," and Auntie Nell spent hours with her, trying to answer the unending questions the child threw at her — chattering, thinking, turning her head on one side like the bird for which she was named.

From a source that Auntie Nell kept secret came money for Lauren. Auntie Nell guarded her with a fierce protectiveness from the vagaries of the streets that teemed with all types of interesting dangers and watched with pride as her young charge grew. Lauren helped Auntie Nell with the secondhand shop she ran on the street and learned about junk and collectibles and antiques.

The funds included college. Lauren, with her analytical mind and her curiosity about all things, did well. The ties between the older woman and the younger loosened, just a little, as Auntie Nell had known they must.

"Time," she told Lauren once, "for the

wrenbird to leave the nest. But I'll be here for you always." There was love — and a hint of tears — in Auntie Nell's voice.

Not always, after all. Within a year after Lauren set up her own small start-up high-tech firm in Silicon Valley, Auntie Nell developed cancer.

The firm did very well indeed.

Nothing else did, though, it seemed to Lauren. She had a small town house that she scarcely saw the inside of, since she spent so much time with her partner, developing and building. And then Dorrie Long, a good friend who seemed tireless in helping build the business, died of an overdose of cocaine.

And Steve Gentry, he of the blond mane of hair and healthclub physique, who wanted to share her town house with her, suddenly seemed to her too goal-oriented, too insensitive, the worst kind of "yuppie."

She talked it over with Auntie Nell, who was battling her cancer with courage and determination. "I've been just like Steve the last year or so, I know that," Lauren admitted. "But with Dorrie dying — and you being sick — things seem all askew. The world seems to have tipped on its axis."

"Burnout?" Auntie Nell knew the right words, though she'd never been susceptible to anything like that in her balanced philosophy.

"I'm tired. I don't like the traffic, or the hectic pace, or the pressure. Once I liked the challenge, but now. . . ."

Auntie Nell became thoughtful, and Lauren noticed with a heart-searing pang that the hollows in her cheeks were more pronounced and that her eyes had lost their brightness. "Let me think, honey. Let me think."

The result of Auntie Nell's thinking was that Lauren took a break and a two-week vacation back to an area of the American landscape she'd never seen before — the hills, rivers, lakes, incredible lushness of the Ozark country.

"You have a distant cousin back there," Auntie Nell told her when she returned feeling as if she were Columbus and had just discovered a New World. "What about trading in your business suit for an antiques shop in southern Missouri?"

It took time, of course. Eventually she sold out most of her interest in her company. She explained to an incredulous Steve Gentry that this was not for her, after all, and that she had to pull up stakes.

Auntie Nell died just before Christmas. Quietly, and with as little fuss as she could manage, she left them, and with her went the last of Lauren's real ties to the Bay Area.

The wrenbird, she told herself, *is ready to migrate.* And with mixed emotions she took flight.

Chapter One

The sign was heavy, being of good, solid pine and about two by three feet. Pops had left it, ready to hang, leaning against the waiting standard and crossbar when he delivered it to her that morning.

Muscles Lauren didn't know she had, plus a streak of dogged determination and the anticipation of seeing the sign in place — these gave her an adrenaline rush that helped ease it into position.

Charlie stood in the long grasses along the fence, tail wagging, head on one side. He looked from her to the newly hung sign and smiled his approving, tongue-lolling Lab smile.

"Dumb dog," she muttered with affection. "No-brain supervisor — but it looks great, doesn't it?"

Charlie picked up his tennis ball and ran off, still smiling.

She backed off and studied the sign, pushing her dark hair from her temples, hunching her shoulders against the muscle tension, tipping her own head to one side much as the dog had done, and with almost the same smile.

Country Blues, the sign said. *Antiques, Folk Art, Collectibles. Lauren Byrd, Prop.* A blue-bandannaed goose marched across the top of the sign, and flowers and grasses cascaded around its feet and down the edges.

Pops had done a wonderful job on it.

Beyond the sign, her smoothly graveled drive led to the wide, low veranda of her shop-and-house. Behind that, pines and oaks climbed the slope of the Missouri hills. *Just like a picture postcard,* she thought, *only better, because it's mine, really mine.*

She closed her eyes momentarily, listening to the near silence. She could hear small birds chirping nearby and a breeze that whispered through the greenly-fresh June grasses. . . .

And a car coming down the two-lane road, heading for town. She paid little attention to the oncoming drone of the engine — until the peace was shattered by the shrieking of brakes, the sound of tires scattering pebbles from the side of the road, Charlie's hysterical barking, and the splintering of wood.

She whirled, every nerve ending bristling. Ready to dive for safety — but which way? Ready to scream, which she did.

"Charlie!" she shrieked. The car had stopped just where the Lab had been romping — no, Charlie was loping across the yard, unhurt.

Lauren swung around to glare at the car, which appeared to have minimal damage. Her rose-covered picket fence beyond the wide gate was a tangled mass of splinters and thorns. A man was opening the driver's door and unfolding himself from the gray sporty sleekness, and he was glaring back at her.

"Your dog," he snapped, dark brows almost meeting in an angry frown. "Why didn't you —"

"My fence," she snarled back. "Couldn't you be more careful?" She took a deep breath. Almost as an afterthought, simply because it was the decent thing to do, she asked, "Are you hurt?"

"I'm fine," he said shortly and looked back at his car. "Dings, thorn scratches, and probably rose petals in the intake valves," he said. "Of the car, I mean."

"It looked so nice." Her voice was tinged with sorrow for the brave early-blooming roses. "The fence, I mean."

The conversation brought a hint of a smile to the man's face, and Lauren felt her tight neck muscles loosening just a bit. She knew who he was, though they'd never been introduced. He was probably the only attorney in this part of the county — Lewis, was it? Or Lucas? She'd been here for six months, but she hadn't had time for socializing, with getting the shop ready to open and getting settled in.

"Your dog ran out onto the highway." The accusatory tone made her give him a sharp look.

"Perhaps you were speeding, and this isn't a speedway."

"Truce," he said in mock surrender, and it was Lauren's turn for a faint smile. "I'm sure my insurance will cover any damages. And there's no permanent harm done."

Lauren glanced toward the veranda. Charlie, with rare discretion, was literally lying low.

"Maybe," she said. "Ten feet more, though, and you'd have had me, my dog, and the new sign too."

"Sorry. Mowing down nice-looking women along the roadside isn't my idea of fun." He glanced toward the sign. "You're Lauren Byrd, aren't you?" It was a statement, not a question; apparently he knew of her, distantly, just as she knew of him. "Great sign — Pops Carmichael's work? When's the official opening?"

"Next week. In time for the tourists."

"We'll have the fence repaired by then. And roses grow fast." He took a card from the slim wallet he'd fished out of his jeans and scribbled on the back of it. "My insurance company.

16

My phone number's on the front. I'll check back with you to make sure everything's all right."

Their hands met briefly as she took the card from him. It seemed to Lauren a curiously intimate touch for something so casual. . . . She took a step backward with the card in her hand, feeling suddenly warm. She couldn't be blushing. There was nothing to blush about, was there? She forced the corners of her mouth into an upward curve and looked up into his eyes.

That ghost of a smile was back on his face, gleaming just faintly from his eyes. It was a face, she thought, that didn't smile easily. There were almost invisible trouble lines on it, shadows behind those changeable hazel eyes. . . .

He was watching her closely too, as if he hadn't really seen her as an individual until that very second. Well, running one's car off the road and into a fence had to be a rather nerve-racking experience. He was handling it quite calmly, all things considered.

He took a deep breath. "Look," he said, "perhaps we were both slightly negligent, but I assure you, I will rectify the situation."

"Excuse me?" Lauren grinned. "You do talk like an attorney, don't you? Besides," she added, looking from him to the fence, "I think you already wrecktified it."

He actually chuckled. "Guess I did, at that. And I didn't mean to sound pompous. I only meant that I'll be sure everything's taken care of."

"I knew what you meant, and I thank you," she said simply, wanting to reach out and touch his arm, for some reason. To reassure him. Instead, she said quickly, "I'm sorry Charlie was out on the road —"

Just as he said, "I'm sorry I wasn't able to stop in time —"

Polite, tentative laughter, and another step apart. "Well," he said, "good luck with your opening. Better keep that dog away from the glassware and customers, though."

She couldn't think of an appropriate rejoinder. Besides, she would be talking to his back, for he had turned and was moving away — easily, with a natural grace, in his loose cotton shirt and expensive stone-washed jeans. Not, she thought wryly, headed for court this afternoon, not in that outfit.

Lauren put the card in her own jeans and started thoughtfully back toward the house, pausing halfway up the drive to look back at her new sign. It was perfect, brave, bright, slightly primitive. How lucky she was to have found Pops!

The sleek, gray sports coupé eased back

onto the roadway and headed on toward town, looking little the worse for its war of the roses.

She couldn't say the same for her fence. She looked toward it and sighed, called Charlie to her side, and went on into the house, taking the card from her pocket. Perry Lucas, it said. Now she remembered. Someone, probably Lily Mae, had said he was from St. Louis, descendant of an early trapper's family. His name was Pierre, wasn't it? Perry fit him better. Nice-looking man. Pity he was a reckless driver.

The "reckless driver" eased his car — a little more slowly now — around the curve beyond and risked a quick glance in the rearview mirror. Well, she was out of sight now — she and the dog both.

It could have been worse. Much worse. He'd heard Lauren Byrd referred to as an "outlander," and he could imagine the sideways, assessing glances of the old-timers. She seemed to be reasonably nice, not too outlandish — for someone from California. Settling comfortably in the Ozarks, if you were from outside, was a challenge at best. And if you came from California, it took more guts than good sense.

Still . . . hadn't he heard that she had relatives or something in the area? That probably helped. Who, though? Well, it didn't really matter.

Antiques and collectibles. . . . A little light bulb suddenly twinkled in the back of his mind. He hadn't even thought to ask her if she had anything to do with steamboats in her stock. He'd have to rectify that.

A slow grin spread over his face and touched his eyes with real amusement. Rectify. He shook his head. He actually did think and talk like a formal nineteenth-century attorney sometimes. Was he turning into a sour old man before his time? Maybe he should rectify *that*. Caroline had been gone for three years now; there were events, people, memories in his past that should stay in the past — if he could just keep them there. Three years could seem forever — or yesterday. Sometimes the past hung about his shoulders like heavy invisible clouds.

But not just now. . . . He switched on the radio and straightened his shoulders because, for some reason, in spite of the accident, he felt almost at peace with himself and his world. Almost.

Looked like rain before the end of the day; there were bruised-looking clouds gathering over the tops of the hills, above the reaching arms of the forest.

He switched his attention back to the car

and the road. No more accidents, please. A short twist of thorny stem seemed to be caught in the chrome toward the front of the fender. "Sorry about that," he told the car and rolled the window down to catch the freshening breezes.

Lauren moved, thoughtful and with a strange mixture of emotions, through the front three "shop" rooms of her house. From here on it was business all the way. Putting her new sign up had been a psychological step: *Hello, world, I'm ready for business.* No more heel-dragging on getting the shop ready to open.

Actually, it had been ready to open for the past two or three weeks. And she could have thrown wide her front door earlier, but she'd been slow. Still rebuilding, she told herself. After all, it was a long way, in both miles and mind-set, from the Silicon Valley to the Ozarks.

With her own countryside field trips, along with the help of two pickers who'd been rec- ommended to her — Dutch Mueller and Harry Johnson — the shop was well stocked. She'd blocked off the front stairway with a handcrafted gate with a pine-tree motif — a work of art in itself. She had the kitchen for her own use, and the back stairway and the three upstairs rooms. She could lie quietly at night, when sleep wouldn't come, and listen to the frogs and the crickets and the quiet night sounds of the woods behind the house.

Now she stood in the midst of her colorful, well-chosen inventory and felt — lost, as if something were missing. She shook herself. There was no reason for this — she'd been feeling so good just a little while before. Everything was just fine. Neither she nor Charlie had been hit, after all. The damage wasn't permanent. Strange, unreadable kind of a man, that Perry Lucas; she hoped he'd be in touch soon. Not that she really wanted to see him, of course, she told herself; she just wanted her fence fixed.

The weather's making me feel addlepated, she thought, walking through a French door that led to a small side porch. *I'm just not used to muggy Missouri summers.* Clouds were building overhead: rich, color-streaked clouds.

"I'm happy, Charlie," she told the dog beside her firmly. "I am very happy, and everything is going to work out."

Circling two or three times, he collapsed on the wood porch floor with an exaggerated sigh. He'd sleep the rest of the afternoon, not caring that he'd almost lost an encounter with a speeding car. *Fine for you to nap,* she thought *wistfully. But what do I do to drive away the barometric doldrums — or whatever this is?*

Ah. She'd call Pops and tell him the sign looked great, that's what. Pops always made the world look better.

His first words proved her right. "Hi, there, little darlin'," he said. "How does it look?" She didn't have to tell him what she was calling about; she seldom did.

And so she told him how wonderful it looked and heard the pride in his voice when he said he hoped it would bring in hordes of antiquers and told her to get her flyers out. "I'm doing another picture for you too. Limestone Creek with fishermen."

"It'll sell," she promised. "You'll be famous someday."

"Better hurry, at my age, hadn't I?"

"Pops, you'll be another Grandma Moses. You're only seventy-six, and she painted into her nineties. You'll be rich *and* famous."

"Then I'll need a whole battery of accountants and tax men and attorneys hassling me all the time. No thanks, honey."

Attorneys. A picture of a gray car entangled with roses and remnants of fence flashed through her mind, along with a startlingly clear picture of the driver of the car — a man with the shadows of pain somewhere deep behind his eyes.

"Lost part of my fence today, Pops — and

23

almost lost Charlie and the sign and myself too," she said in an abrupt change of subject. She related the story, feeling some of the same emotions she had felt standing there earlier in the sun with the fence, and the torn roses, and the disquieting man. "He's a little strange, very quiet. Well, I hope his insurance comes through, anyway."

"Glad you're okay, but don't worry, darlin'. If the insurance company starts fencing with you — oh, I didn't mean that as a pun, but all right, there it is — Perry will take care of it himself. He's that kind."

"I hope you're right. He doesn't smile much, does he?"

"Would you be smiling if you'd just run your car into a picket fence? True, he does tend to be a tad glum sometimes, but he's gone through some bad times in the past few years — lost his wife, worked himself to a frazzle, and had to get away from St. Louis to keep his sanity. If I remember right, he was an up-and-coming assistant district attorney. Sad situation."

"Yes," Lauren said, thoughtful. "Still . . . I guess I'll just feel better when that fence is mended."

"Oh, well, those things almost always work out, mostly, sometimes, seems like." And with that typical Pops Carmichael statement, he excused himself to get back to his canvas and brushes.

Pops was special. Sometimes Lauren wondered about his "down-home" way of talking; he wasn't a native, she knew that, but he was reticent about his past. She suspected there was a lot more to Pops than she knew. He'd been here nearly fifteen years, retired, happy, he said, as a woodchuck in a lumberyard.

Lauren leaned against the kitchen window frame, looking out at the green slope behind the house, now a duller green under darkening skies. It was probably just the fault of the falling barometer, but there was still that feeling of listlessness — almost a sadness — clinging around her with an almost tangible weight. Talking to Pops had helped, but only momentarily.

She should be so happy. She'd left the rat race behind, had done exactly what she wanted to do, and would officially open her shop soon. Whistling or singing would be more appropriate than moping, surely. She tried to whistle, hummed a few bars of "Camptown Races," and gave it up as the notes fell thin and flat in the silence of the house.

The Drunkard's Path quilt was a bit askew on the back of the oak Victorian church pew. Straightening it brought a small smile. The combination of pew and quilt pleased her;

the quilt made her think of its maker. Lily Mae. Would she possibly have a cup of common sense and herbal tea to share on a broody afternoon?

"Well, 'course, honey, always do for you, don't I? 'Sakes, you sound lower than a snake's belly. Get yourself down here, and I'll fix you up with tea and oatmeal cookies and show you the Log Cabin quilt I'm working on. Hurry, now, afore it starts to rain."

Lauren put the phone down and hurried. A visit with Lily Mae would be fine medicine. And she wanted to see that new quilt. She even managed a weak "doo-dah" as she shot out the back door.

"Watch the house, Charlie," she called back to the dog. Charlie raised his head an inch, woofed, and went back to sleep. *Fine watchdog*, she thought. *Glad this is a low-crime area.*

Three miles up the winding road that eased lazily and bumpily away from the lake, away, somehow, from the twentieth century — Lauren came to the Compton cabin. Old, neat, it nestled comfortably under an ancient hickory. Built by Lily Mae's grandfather before the turn of the century, the cabin with its silvery-gray clapboards gleamed a welcome even on a dull afternoon.

And Lily Mae, a fine-boned, bright-eyed little bird of a woman, had heard her coming and was standing on the porch with a smile that intensified the welcome tenfold.

"Thank heavens for you and Pops," Lauren said, giving the older woman a quick hug.

Lily Mae hugged her back and then pushed her away, looking up at her shrewdly. "You got sadness in your heart, child? Come have tea and talk, then, and we'll get things untangled."

By the time Lauren had eased herself into a chair at the pale scrubbed-pine table in the kitchen, she already felt better. The cinnamon-spiced aroma of freshly baked oatmeal cookies hung in the air, and she felt herself relaxing.

"I'm fine, really," Lauren said, not too convincingly. "Had kind of a busy afternoon — needed some cookies and company, that's all." "Busy" wasn't really quite the right word; she wondered what word Perry Lucas might choose for their encounter.

"That right?" Lily Mae put a mug of tea that smelled of lemon and mint in front of Lauren and hoisted her eyebrows a half inch. "More to it than that, I'd reckon. You're too wrapped up in that shop, and you're feeling lonesome and a little homesick. Not natural, a pretty young thing like you being alone so much."

Of course, she hadn't been alone all afternoon, Lauren thought. Unexpected company had burst upon her, after all. . . .

A cookie melted into delicious warm crumbs between Lauren's lips, and she came close to purring. "Perfect," she said when she could talk. "But no — I'm not lonely. I have Charlie." She ignored Lily Mae's snort. "And home is here now, so I can't be homesick. Besides, I'm not that pretty, and I'm not that young." A tiny corner of her psyche twitched; that seemed too true.

"Twenty-seven's not old, and you've got the prettiest gray eyes I ever saw." Lily Mae thumped her cup down and shook her head. "You need to get out so more people see 'em, that's all."

"I'll see plenty of customers over the summer, I hope. Won't that count? Tourists, but still —"

"Tourists are all right, long as they come through with money in their pockets. There are necessary evils in life. But what about the young men? Like Nelson Hawke, out at the lake, or that young doctor from Boone's Knob —"

"I'm going to sit around and vegetate forever," Lauren assured Lily Mae solemnly, "getting old and rusticating away. . . ."

"I'm not sure, exactly, what those words mean, but horsefeathers," Lily Mae snapped.

Then, "Come see the quilt. It's all in the prettiest lights and darks. It's coming alive."

It was. "For my shop?" Lauren asked.

"Or your hope chest," Lily Mae answered meaningfully.

A few drops of rain spattered tentatively against the windows, and Lily Mae eased them closed, scanning the sky with a practiced weather eye. "Just a teaser. Won't amount to a hill of beans, but we'll have a beautiful sunset. You should go up to Glade Ridge and watch it with someone like Nels Hawke."

"Lily Mae, you have a stubborn, one-track mind," Lauren said, laughing. It was, she thought, the first time she'd really laughed all afternoon.

"That's better." Lily Mae in many ways was about the closest thing she could get to another Auntie Nell, though physically they were so different, and they lived in different worlds. A momentary feeling of loss, of grief, passed over Lauren, erasing the laughter.

And Lily Mae caught the change of mood and countered it by an abrupt change of subject. "I'm going to make you something I think you'll like." She waved her hands at the supply shelves beside her. "Last time Dutch and Harry stopped by your place, they brought me some bolt ends they'd picked up with some other things in a lot at auction —

just for me, they said." Her nose crinkled a little. "If those two old goats were any fuller of hot air, they'd float right off into the clouds. They just didn't know what to do with the stuff. But I been thinking . . . I could make you an awful pretty one of those things you like — caftans, is that it? Be really special, wouldn't it?"

"It would be, Lily Mae," she said softly. Wearing caftans was a way she could keep a tenuous tie to her mother's memory.

"Well, with your height, they look good on you. Funny-looking garments, but I'll do one for you, child."

Lauren's smile came fully awake. "Thank you. How can I repay you?"

"Just keep bringing me those extra old canning jars you get from time to time. They come in real handy."

The halfhearted storm had passed on, leaving the late afternoon fresh and cooled. "Guess I should get home," Lauren said. "Sit on the porch and contemplate nature and get myself in tune with the universe on such a beautiful evening."

"Well, you *could* go up to Hawke's Nest and see if you can get him away from that resort of his for a nice little drive — on such a beautiful evening. Now, that might get you in tune with the universe, whatever that means, *real* quick."

"Lily Mae!"

"Can't help it. I'm an interfering old woman." She followed Lauren out onto the small porch, folding over the top of a brown paper bag full of cookies. "Take these, now, and cheer up." Lauren dutifully looked cheerful.

Lily Mae nodded, as if to herself. "Just one thing, long as you're feeling a little more chipper — something I heard in town this morning."

A tiny instinctive warning light flashed at the back of Lauren's mind. Small-town grapevines are better — or at least quicker — than instant satellite coverage. "What is it?"

"It's that fool Ernie Campbell next door to you, honey. He has some kind of bee in his bonnet, idiot man. How Lou's put up with him all these years, I don't know."

"Lily Mae," Lauren said quietly, "what kind of bee?"

"Well, he says your new parking lot laps over on his land, takes out ten feet or so that's his, and he says he'll raise Cain —"

"But that's ridiculous! I have all the papers, the deeds, the easements — everything. If he thought I was encroaching on his land, why didn't he say so before?"

"Encroaching. I like that word. . . . He's

31

just ornery, Lauren. But, you know — might be wise to talk to a lawyer. Just one around I know of, and that's Perry Lucas."

Lauren sighed. Perry Lucas seemed to have entered her life in a totally disrupting way in just one day.

Well, she'd met tougher challenges. She was no idiot: She'd developed and run a successful business, and she had her life firmly under control. She'd handle it. *Keep telling yourself that, Lauren Byrd,* she told herself silently.

But a little of the luster had faded from the beauty of the June evening as she drove back to Country Blues. And it seemed destined to dim still further, both literally and figuratively. The westering sun had hidden its glow behind yet another cloud, a bosomy stray trailing behind others now sailing their way east. The fine gravel of her parking lot glistened damply.

So did the garbage dump of junk — there was no other word for it — that had been scattered along the edge of the parking lot just inside her neat white boundary fence.

Chapter Two

Lauren jerked her van to a halt and just sat for a moment, staring.

Then she reached into the brown paper bag and took out two cookies, eating them slowly and concentrating on good, uplifting thoughts like Lily Mae, Pops, and spicy cookies — and Charlie. Where was Charlie? He hadn't come romping noisily to meet her. For a few seconds panic almost overtook her.

But there he was. Under the tree, stretched out lazily, smiling at her — a smile that said, *Well, hey, sorry, but I couldn't do anything about it.*

She growled. He smiled. She started on another cookie.

Apparently the junk — old tires, brush, an unsightly collection of cans and bottles, some unidentifiable masses that she didn't think she wanted to investigate too closely — had been thrown over from the other side of the fence.

Ernie Campbell's side of the fence.

She stifled a primal scream and eased her van into the garage at the back of the lot. Charlie wouldn't have created much of a ruckus at the dumping. He was somewhat used to Ernie, though Ernie wasn't exactly neighborly. Obviously.

Their houses were widely spaced. Ernie owned the sporting-goods store and worked on outboard motors in his spare time. She knew him to say hello to, but neither he nor his wife had done much to make her welcome in Piney Ridge.

Not many of the townspeople, the "natives," had been very friendly. So far. Maybe with time. . . .

Lauren sighed, took cookies and emotions in hand and headed for the house. Charlie followed behind — several paces, as befitted a dog who sensed he hadn't quite measured up to expectations.

Should she call Ernie? Throw the responsibility squarely in his lap? If only she could do the same with the mess! Of course, he'd deny it. Or would he tell her that since that edge of the parking lot wasn't hers, he could darned well do what he pleased?

She marched into the house, anger and indecision making her, unintentionally, slam the door in Charlie's already woebegone face. "Sorry," she mumbled and opened the door for him just as the phone in her kitchen jangled sharply. *Like my nerves,* she thought. *What next?*

Dumping keys and bags on the counter, she

answered impatiently to find that "what next" was a smooth and apologetic voice that seemed to sense her mood. Perry Lucas's voice.

"Sorry if I disturbed you. I probably took you away from something?"

What he had taken her away from was not something she wanted to think about.

"It's quite all right," she said through teeth that were still gritted with frustration and anger. It was difficult. Wasn't he, really, part of her problems?

He spoke swiftly, as if trying to rush the words out before she could hang up on him. "I just wanted to tell you that I've already contacted my insurance company," he said. "Thing is, it being Friday, I'm not sure how soon they'll act. And I know you're opening soon and want to get it repaired quickly."

She sighed deeply. "It just can't be helped, can it?" At least he was trying. "I suppose it won't deter any customers. It was difficult to be fair and rational, and her tone of voice showed it.

"I'll see what I can do to hurry things, Miss Byrd. Perhaps I can expedite matters a bit."

A hint of a giggle underlaid her polite thank you and goodbye. He was sounding like a nineteenth-century barrister again — odd little formalities of speech that served to distance him from the immediate problem. *A defense mechanism?* she wondered fleetingly.

The fence, the roses, the junk in her parking lot — those were *her* immediate problems. She made a sandwich and took it out to the porch, Charlie dogging her heels in hopes of a left-over. "Fat chance," she told him, and tried to think. But she hardly tasted her sandwich, and even sitting on the front porch staring at her new sign didn't give her much joy.

"Poor roses," she muttered aloud. Charlie whined and looked hopefully at the remains of the sandwich. She gave it to him absently and went into the house.

She'd have to call Ernie Campbell. She would choose her words with care, but she couldn't just let him get away with it.

"You saw him, didn't you, Charlie? You could identify him, right?" Charlie smiled his agreeable smile.

"Bah," she told him disgustedly and looked up Ernie's number in the small phone book that hung beside her kitchen wall phone.

"Oh, yes, Miss Byrd," Lou Campbell said in her soft, somewhere-else voice. "Ernie's out back. I'll get him for you?" Lou Campbell ended most sentences with uncertain question marks.

"Please," Lauren answered firmly and pressed her lips together tightly, waiting.

Ernie's voice, when he came to the phone,

seemed to her to have a slight mocking tone in it. "Yeah, Miss Byrd," he said. "Something I can do for you?"

"I just wondered," she said as evenly as she could, "if you knew anything about a — a mess of litter that was left in my parking lot sometime this afternoon."

He laughed a somewhat unpleasant laugh. "A mess of litter, huh? On the parking lot. Well, now." He paused, but she said nothing. Let him answer. "Well, now," he repeated. "Maybe some wild kids from the city, maybe just someone who wanted to get rid of some old junk and stuff and thought an antiques store was a good place for it. Maybe."

"You didn't hear or see anyone, then?" He'd deny it.

He denied it. But then he said, " 'Course, you realize that edge of your parking lot along that fancy fence of yours is actually on my land. Maybe you should move the fence over some?"

Lauren paused and then let a smile come into her voice. "Gotcha, Ernie Campbell," she said agreeably. "How did you know exactly where the, er, litter was dumped?"

With great effort she managed to hang up the phone very softly on the bluster that crackled along the wires. No sense in breaking the phone, after all. She was tired, angry, depressed.

Sleep came slowly that night. Sitting at her open bedroom window, rocking in the old wicker chair she'd picked up in St. Louis, she looked out over the starlit yard. For at least the hundredth time she asked herself, *Have I done the right thing, coming here, transplanting myself into a new life, a new world?*

The answer, she decided, was yes. Eventually she slept, though her dreams were troubled.

The morning, Lauren observed with half-open eyes, was bright and full of slanting sun rays. They flooded through the window and the lace curtains, patterning the room with a lovely light.

She stretched, yawned, opened her eyes fully, remembered the day before, and closed them again.

Charlie was barking in the kitchen. She opened her eyes and peered at the clock. How could it be eight-thirty? She *never* slept until eight-thirty. But it *was* eight-thirty.

What was Charlie "creating" about, as Lily Mae would ask? Groping for her slippers and robe, she padded to the window.

A truck was parked on the road shoulder, and there were two — three? — men and a load of lumber. And an expensive gray car parked ahead of the truck, and a dark-haired man talking and gesturing intently — a man with broad shoulders that were covered today with a chambray workshirt with the sleeves rolled up.

Her eyes fully open now, she made short work of donning chinos, shirt, and sandals. She was in and out of the big old-fashioned bathroom in record time, and she and Charlie both shot out the side door faster than speeding bullets.

Charlie made a great deal more noise about it than she did, which gained the attention of the men beside the road.

"*Good* morning," Perry Lucas greeted her. "Thought you'd never notice us. Didn't want to disturb you too much, too early —"

"Already?" she interrupted him, attention divided between Perry's half smile and the two men unloading fence posts, concrete mix, and diggers. "Already? Who carries your insurance? I'm impressed. I'm switching. I don't believe it."

"That's smart — not believing it, I mean. I'm getting a head start on the company, since you're opening so soon. They can settle with me later. Will that be" — his eyes twinkled — "sufficient rectification? Though I can't make the roses grow back by next week.

Brown thumbs."

Lauren glanced down at his hands. Large, capable, well-kept hands — without brown thumbs. *I'm still dreaming,* she thought.

"Thank you. I didn't expect such — such immediate action."

He made a little mocking bow. "It was the least I could do."

"Thank you again. Look — I haven't made coffee yet. I'll make a big pot if you think — if you'd all like —"

One of the men unloading lumber gave her a gap-toothed grin that said coffee sounded great, and the twinkle reappeared in Perry's eyes. His eyes were nice when they twinkled, she thought; it drove the shadows away.

"Wonderful," he said. "May I use your phone? I want to call the car agency in Springfield and see if they have touch-up paint for the car. There's one little spot I can't rub out."

"Of course. I'm so sorry," she answered before she could remind herself that it hadn't been *her* fault, after all, that his car had spots. "The phone's in the kitchen."

He stopped abruptly behind her, staring at the parking lot, before she could swing the porch screen open. "Good heavens. Is that a new branch of the Piney Ridge dump?"

"Not intentionally," she said grimly. "Look,

I'll make the coffee, and you make your call, and then I'll tell you about it."

He finally located just the right shade of paint, and she located her large coffee maker, which she figured she'd need, judging from the size of the two workmen. After she'd carried out a tray with huge steaming mugs for them, she settled Perry Lucas across from her at the table by her kitchen window. She even shared the last of Lily Mae's cookies with him, which she thought was an uncommonly friendly gesture.

He seemed to think so too, judging from the beatific smile that lit his features as he finished off two of them with scarcely a deep breath. But, almost immediately, his face fell into its normally solemn lines. *Pity,* she thought, *as if the sun's gone under a cloud.*

He leaned forward, leveling a disconcertingly cool look at her. "Now, Miss Byrd, about the, er, debris?"

She wanted to kick him, tickle him, anything to chase the stiff reserve away. "My name is Lauren," she said. "And I think my problem is Ernie Campbell, though it would be hard to prove."

She told him the story, starting with Lily Mae's warning and ending with her phone conversation with Ernie. "If he had any problems with my buying this place, why didn't he say so before? What suddenly got into him, anyway?"

Perry shook his head, looking somewhere between exasperation and amusement. "Cussedness. It didn't get into him suddenly — he was born with it. He's always been ornery. You're from 'outside.' It probably took him a while to dream up some reason for being obnoxious. I can double-check the old land records to make sure you're right. I'm sure you are, in spite of the fact that you're from California."

"Now wait just a minute —"

"That's not my thinking. It's Ernie's. His orneriness takes its time surfacing sometimes. He realized that you really were here to stay, and he finally reacted."

"I had no problem getting permission to open my shop." Her voice bristled with indignation. Why couldn't she sound cooler, more businesslike?

"It's not the shop," he said soothingly. "This house was built about 1902 by the Pennyfeathers. Old Ben Pennyfeather was like an uncle to Ernie, and when Ben died last year, Ernie lost both a neighbor and a good friend. Ernie probably started to think that you were undoubtedly a hippie bringing in drugs and a sinful commune of some kind right next door to him. People who've been here for generations sometimes have an exaggerated view of Californians, you know."

"I'm not some spaced-out —" she started, feeling hurt welling up in her, plus a resentment that mushroomed from her memories of her mother and her childhood. "I'm not like that."

"I know that." His voice was calm, but she could hear the curiosity about her flaring defensiveness. "Now look, don't worry. I'll check into it, and all that junk — well, we could get on Ernie's case, but why give him the satisfaction? I'll just have Duane and Pete load it all up in their truck and cart it out to the dump when they're done with the fence. We'll deal with Ernie later."

She looked at Perry for a long, quiet moment before nodding reluctantly. He certainly had a lot of "we's" in there.

"I appreciate your help," she said at last.

"It's a pleasure," he answered somewhat formally, and then his face lit up with a rare, real smile as he seemed to think of something that was even more of a pleasure.

"What I saw of your shop as we came in — you have an impressive stock. Do you happen to have anything to do with steamboats?"

"Steamboats? Steamboats. You mean —"

"I mean steamers, paddlewheelers, sternwheelers, sidewheelers — anything that pertains to them, from scale models to posters. I am," he added unnecessarily, "a steamboat nut. Dreamed, when I was a kid, of piloting one. A Mark Twain complex, I guess."

Lauren grinned and stood up. "Come on," she told him. "You can have a guided pre-opening tour. Though the only thing I can think of that you might be interested in is a gorgeous old photo of Mark Twain himself — probably original. It's nice."

They moved companionably among the generous clutter of old things that had "spoken" to Lauren and asked for a chance at a new life. He seemed impressed by the variety and asked knowledgeable questions, including one that made her wince a bit.

"Do you have trouble picking things up locally?"

"Yes, to be honest. The natives aren't too willing to part with their antiques when an outsider starts asking. I rely on Harry Johnson and Dutch Mueller — they're pickers, kind of middlemen."

"I know them, yes. Maybe I could help you out now and then — I know everyone within thirty miles. I grew up here, though I lived in St. Louis until last year." The cloud crossed behind his eyes again, and he turned from her. "Mark Twain?" he asked.

"Over here." She reached inside a drop-front desk and pulled out an old gessoed frame with a snapshot in it. He glanced at the price tag, nodded, and looked pleased.

"Your first sale. And keep me in mind, won't you? If you run into anything to do with steamboats, I mean."

"Of course — but please, just take the picture." A tiny inner voice scolded her, telling her that wasn't very businesslike, but she shut it out. He was helping her, and he was a nice, if rather dour, man, wasn't he?

He started to argue with her, but she shook her head with finality and a friendly smile, and he thanked her. "And now I should get out and check on how Duane and Pete are doing — and ask them to cart off that junk. Thank you again. I'll talk to you as soon as I check out all the legal deeds to that land."

"I should thank *you*," Lauren said. Something deep in her soul, her heart, her intuition, told her that she just might have a new and capable friend. Reserved, oddly aloof — but a friend. Her list of friends here was, thank heavens, growing — slowly.

"One thing," Perry said as he headed out onto her porch. "Just a technical question about antiques —"

"Ask away," Lauren said, ready to explain the fine points of the antiques business.

"Who the heck" — he made a sweeping

gesture around the crowded shop with his left hand, and there was a smile in his eyes — "who the heck *dusts* all this stuff, anyway?"

Who the heck, indeed, Lauren thought wryly two hours later, putting her lamb's-wool duster away. That was a question people rarely had in mind when they looked at the fascinating clutter of a good antiques store. There was polishing, refurbishing, refinishing — and always, talking soothingly to all these inanimate objects, a habit she'd picked up from Auntie Nell. "Helps transform an old piece that thinks it's junk into a self-respecting antique if it's talked to nicely," she'd said.

There really wasn't any reason why that sort of attitude should make a difference, but somehow it did. And down in the cellar now was a small pine table with worn paint that needed a good talking to.

Lauren turned on the light over the table and started to work with fine steel wool, crooning to the table encouragingly.

Pops had found the table at a yard sale, bless him. He'd stopped by for the first time on an Ozark spring day, when the world was greening up and the buds were swelling — a day when she just *had* to get out and paint the window boxes on her porch.

He'd pulled his pickup into her drive, introduced himself, and stayed to wield a brush with efficient flourishes. They'd been friends ever since. He'd introduced her to Lily Mae, picked up small items for her — and, of course, there were his paintings.

She buffed the oiled finish of the table and carried it upstairs to position it, just so, near the door. Should she put a burl bowl on it? That redware charger or —

The telephone interrupted her reverie.

"Good afternoon, gorgeous," a familiar deep voice said. "How does roast prime rib sound for dinner this evening? Or fresh-caught catfish? Or" — there was a pause, as if a menu were being consulted, which was probably the case — "perhaps Southern baked ham, with a moonlit ride over the lake afterward? Oh, and I have some fantastic ideas for dessert —"

"Nelson," Lauren said, laughing, "slow down. Are you inviting me out to Hawke's Nest for dinner?"

"Dinner, a ride on the lake, and about that dessert —"

"Not on my diet, Mr. Hawke," she said primly. She liked Nelson Hawke — his bantering, his easygoing attitude. He never seemed put out by her refusal of his romantic overtures — she suspected he didn't really mean them, anyway. Or did he?

A sudden vivid picture — the contrast of Nelson Hawke's easy laughter and the sadness in Perry Lucas's eyes — passed across her mind. She told Nels that the baked ham sounded wonderful and, shaking her head slightly to clear away that picture, went upstairs to take a shower.

Chapter Three

After making sure the reconstruction work was well under way at Country Blues, Perry stopped for lunch, ran a few errands, and headed home to his glowing Carpenter's Gothic house. It welcomed him from under aged sycamores, fretwork and scrolls spanking white where the sunlight pierced through the leaves and made shadows dance over the facade.

It felt good to come home, more and more so these days. It was reassuring; this house had been a second home to him, after all, when he was a boy and his grandparents still lived there.

There were only three messages on his answering machine. Joseph Morrison wanted to change his will again, something he did every time his son displeased (or pleased) him. A woman in Lakeville was seeking power of attorney. A boy outside town was in trouble with the law for the third time and wanted his advice. . . .

If it weren't for the huge number of summer people and retirees, Perry thought, he really wouldn't have enough to do — enough to keep his mind busy, occupied, away from the ghosts and clinging wraiths of the past. And that was very important.

He carried the picture of Mark Twain that Lauren had given him into his office, smiling a little — whether at the picture or at the thought of Lauren Byrd, he wasn't quite sure. It had been a long time since he'd found any woman worth thinking twice about. And he couldn't, wouldn't start now.

He stood for a moment looking around. His office — remodeled from two rooms into one — was overcrowded. Almost, he thought, like Lauren's shop. But at least he had a house-keeper to come in once a week to dust over the tops of things.

Where to put the photo?

On top of a low bookcase between two windows there might be room — there was an old shaving mug with a steamboat transfer and the name *Grand Lady* — and his studio portrait of Caroline. He stood and looked at it achingly, motionless. He still missed her.

Walking over to the bookcase, he put the Mark Twain photograph beside Caroline's. "Hi," he said. "Thought you'd like some good company." He reached out, one finger lightly tracing the golden hair that was caught forever over one shoulder.

Lauren Byrd has hair like that, he thought,

with that soft wave, but hers is dark. He turned away to go sit behind his desk.

The old office chair tilted back comfortably. He relaxed, hands behind his head, and surveyed his favorite room. One wall was taken up by a massive pilot's wheel. His ornate chandelier, his client chairs, his decorations were from long-gone steamboats; the soporific warmth of the curtain-filtered afternoon sunlight settled around him. With eyes almost closed, he half dreamed.

He was at the wheel in the pilot house. The river stretched ahead of him, its edges mistily blurred. Light glimmered on the waters far ahead. The voice of the leadsman taking the soundings floated back to him, faint, from another age: "Maark twaaiin. . . ."

But the euphoric peace lasted only a moment. The roughly clad leadsman turned to look at him, grimy, grinning face suddenly magnified and looming close until it covered his entire field of vision. He knew it too well, that pugnacious, accusing face.

Jolted into wakefulness, he willed the face away. His peace had once again been shattered, as it so often was.

On Monday, Perry made a trip to the county seat to take care of a couple of things that needed his attention. *Might as well,* he thought, *double-check the old boundary records for Lauren, make copies of all the pertinent papers, plan to have a quiet talk with Ernie Campbell.*

Why, he chided himself, was he becoming so involved with her problems? Because he felt slightly guilty about her fence? Because she had given him a picture of Mark Twain? Or was it more? Whatever it was, he'd promised he'd check, and he would.

Three hours later his neck was stiff, his eyes slightly bleary, and his mind full of even more unanswered questions. Frowning, he went back to the counter where Mavis Loring presided over the record archives.

No, she assured him firmly, there was nothing more on that parcel of land. And if Mavis said that was it, that was it.

Perry went back to his table and sat down and stared at the yellowing documents in front of him. Somewhere along the line there had been a transposition of numbers. Twenty-three feet had become thirty-two feet. Ernie Campbell appeared to be right.

But if Ernie knew about this, why hadn't he said anything before?

Perry could make a guess at that — fathers and grandfathers might have stumbled on the fact years before, laughed about the natural stupidity of county officials, and amiably shared their boundaries. Ernie had heard the old stories, probably even forgetting about them. Until Lauren Byrd moved in next door to him and his natural distrust of outlanders — especially feisty females from California — brought it back to mind.

Lauren wasn't going to like this. Not at all.

Lauren brushed her long hair back, down, stroke after stroke, until it gleamed darkly, the shade of the antique mirror's mahogany frame. She peered at her image. Wear it loose today? Or a ponytail? Finally she decided on a heavy sleek side braid that fell smoothly to her breast. The gray eyes in the mirror looked back at her with approval. That would do.

She slipped her arms through the flowing sleeves of the paisley caftan in rich muted shades of browns and ivories. Now the ivory disc earrings. That would do too.

I should put on jeans and dig in the cellar, she scolded her reflection, *and wax that old sideboard and sand the pine nightstand. But not today. Not my last day of real freedom.*

She'd hung the Closed Mondays notice on the bottom of her sign at dusk on Sunday and admired the restored fence. Even the roses were recovering; the damage had been "rectified" very well.

She slipped almost noiselessly down her

stairs, made coffee, put out a bowl of water for Charlie, thought about breakfast — and remembered that she'd meant to call Pops first thing.

"My, don't you look pretty!" was the first thing he said. "Don't tell me I can't see you — I have a good imagination. What gets you up so early today?"

"News," she said. "Good news. A surprise. Your sign's already working, Pops — five or six cars stopped yesterday afternoon, thanks to you. In spite of a notice on the porch that the 'Grand Opening' would be on Tuesday."

"And of course you let them in. Good. Browsers or buyers?"

"Both — just curious, mostly, but I sold a set of yellowware bowls, and a Toby mug, a-a-and —" She drew the word out, teasing him. "And your picture of the old Woodhill Church. For four hundred and fifty dollars. Paint faster, Grandpa Moses. It's just beginning."

"Lordy! Folks must have more money than taste. And you get — lessee — one hundred and fifty of that, right?"

"Right. And I have a bare spot on my wall that needs filling. Quick."

"This evening quick enough? You may have to put a 'wet paint' sign on it, but — Wonderful start for the shop, honey." She could

54

hear the pleasure and pride in his voice, though he was trying to sound offhand.

"Good start for you too," she told him. "See you later."

She took coffee cup and clipboard and pencil out to the shady side porch. Charlie lumbered up and plopped contentedly beside her. Bird song and peace filled the air. "I'm happy, Charlie, and everything is going to work out perfectly," she told the dog. Those words sounded much more convincing to her than when she'd said almost the same thing on Friday afternoon.

An hour later she had a long list of "wants" for Harry and Dutch and sat back, rocking contentedly in the old porch rocker. Even glancing over at the disputed area of the parking lot didn't bother her; they'd clear up the misunderstanding. The fence was fixed, the flowers were growing, Pops's paintings were selling, and the world was beautiful. Nothing could spoil things now.

Perry made copies of pertinent papers, took notes, and left the mustiness of the old courthouse behind, feeling a little grim.

How would he explain all this to Lauren? And when? He frowned, looking at his watch. Might as well get it over with. There was time to drop the bombshell in Lauren's lap before lunch and try to smooth things — but how? And it wasn't even his problem, after all. As he drove back to Piney Ridge, his mind went in circles.

Admit it. You'd hoped to play the superhero role, rescuing the damsel in distress — and now you're just going to give her more distress. And — admit it — you were looking forward to seeing her again, right?

Maybe. But not like this.

He pulled into the driveway at Country Blues, and that darned fool of a dog greeted him with friendly eyes at the front steps — probably a lot friendlier than Lauren's would be when he gave her the news. He gave the old-fashioned doorbell a tweak, heard it jangle, heard her call out a cheery "Coming!" He steeled himself.

And darn it, she looked genuinely glad to see him. He obediently stepped into the shop when she told him to and promptly forgot whatever it was that he was going to say next. She stood, just a few feet away, staring at him curiously. He stared back, mute. Her image seemed to fill his entire soul.

Her strong chin tilted up slightly, expectantly, only an inch or so beneath his own. He hadn't realized she was so tall. And those cheekbones, and the gray eyes, and that smile that was beginning to fade as she waited for him to speak. . . .

That long, thick braid of hair — the end of it curled just slightly, alive and caressing, on her shoulder. The graceful folds of fabric that surrounded her, chin to floor, seemed to suggest and delineate the grace of her. She was beautiful. . . . He had to say something and say it quickly. She had already taken a step back from him, a puzzled look in her eyes.

"Sorry," he said, surprised that his voice sounded almost normal. "Sun blindness, I think. Took a minute to adjust." He blinked his eyes rapidly to underscore this offering.

The corners of her mouth lifted again. "I understand," she said, and he had the terrible feeling that she really did.

He raised the hand that held his notes and papers, looked at it with distaste, and let it fall back to his side. "I've done some research on Ernie Campbell's claim. Very interesting. Quite a bit of conflicting data." There. He was in control again.

"Come into the kitchen," she offered, "and have some coffee with me. Um — conflicting data?"

He swallowed. "There are things — er, a few small details." Why couldn't he just say that Ernie had a pretty good case?

"I understand," she said again in the same way. "Well." She handed him his coffee. "Maybe we'd better take a look?"

He lifted his hand again, looked at the papers, looked at his watch. "I know," he said, inspired. "It's almost lunchtime. May I take you to Jenny's Cafe for a sandwich? I can tell you all about it there." His nerves and emotions were beginning to return to normal. He could probably be quite rational again in a public place like Jenny's. . . .

Lauren gave him another of her long looks. "That's very nice of you," she said finally. "Yes, I'd like that. Just let me get my keys, and I'll be ready —" The caftan swirled around her as she turned from him.

"Like that?" he asked incredulously, appalled at the words he heard coming out of his mouth. "I mean, aren't you going to get dressed first?"

She looked down at her caftan, up at his troubled eyes, and burst into laughter. "I *am* dressed," she said, "but maybe not for Piney Ridge."

She was still chuckling, changing into a brown cotton skirt and shirtwaist. Had he really thought she was still in her robe at midday? No — he had to be joking.

Although he was right. The ladies of Piney

Ridge didn't wear caftans to Jenny's Café for lunch. Tourists might, but not a resident. Unless the resident were very strange — outlandish? Like the new antiques dealer at Country Blues. She winced.

A braid, now, should be acceptable. She smoothed it as she hurried back down the stairs. An uneasy question stirred: Was he hedging on the matter of the property line? If so, why? Stopping for a moment midstairs, she tried to gather her thoughts.

Perry was acting very strange. For a minute there she'd thought he was reacting to her as a man might react to a woman he suddenly sees as desirable, but perhaps she was flattering herself and he'd just been ill at ease because he had bad news.

Her smile was forced by the time she re-entered the kitchen.

His, by contrast, was real and warm. "You look wonderful," he said easily. "You did before too, and I'm sorry if I implied otherwise." He was falling back into his formal speech patterns.

"You don't have to apologize," she told him. "I understood what you were thinking."

Momentarily he looked as if this statement, too, had made him uneasy, but then he relaxed. "Jenny makes a great BLT."

She nodded. "I know. I've been there. In

jeans," she added and called Charlie into the house.

She asked no questions on the way to Jenny's. *Let him tell it in his own time,* she thought a little apprehensively.

He piled all the papers on the Formica tabletop when they'd ordered. "Do I have to read all those?" she asked warily.

"No. Nobody could, anyway, and tackle one of Jenny's BLTs." Which was a juicy truth. He took a deep breath. "A mistake was made a long time ago. I'm sorry."

"You didn't make it?"

"Of course not."

"Then don't apologize. Are you trying to say that Ernie was — or is — right, after all?" She suddenly wanted to punch someone, preferably Ernie Campbell, though she tried to stay calm.

"I wish it weren't so," Perry said quietly.

"So do I." She stared disconsolately at him. "So do I."

A movement at the counter caught her eye. A hand raised in greeting — Nels. She gave him a quick, forced smile. Nels could put so much meaning into one raised eyebrow, and he did so now, looking curiously from her to Perry. She watched him pay for his iced tea and stride toward the door. She looked back at Perry.

60

"And just what do I do now?" she asked.

"Besides wiping the mayonnaise off your chin? Nothing, as far as Ernie is concerned. Let him bring it up again. And in the meantime I'll do some more checking."

"If the mistake was made long ago, maybe the — what? — statute of limitations has run out, or something? Since I bought the property in good faith and without challenge?"

"Something like that," he said without much conviction.

"Well. Thank you for checking," she said grudgingly.

"My pleasure," he said, though his face reflected little pleasure. "Oh, you know what I mean. It's my thanks for that picture you gave me, partly." He stared somberly at her, then out the window, then back, as if trying to make a momentous decision.

"You have Pops's paintings and Lily Mae's quilts," he said. "Are you interested in the work of a genuine Ozark wood carver?"

Lauren had long since developed a sixth sense about antiques and folk art — antennae, Auntie Nell had called them, that could pick up promising vibes. Those antennae went straight up now and quivered excitedly. "You know one — one who might do business with an outlander?"

"Yup. 'Way up in the hills — a friend of

my grandfather's. I could take you up there. It might be advantageous if I were with you, since he knows me pretty well." Why was he doing this?

"Thursday," she said. "I don't open until one on Thursday. That is — well, if you have the time on Thursday?"

"Thursday it is," he told her and picked up the lunch check.

That evening, bare feet propped on a Victorian footstool, she relaxed lazily in her bedroom. A documentary went half watched on TV, and Charlie snored gently at her side.

Perry was almost a challenge, with that odd reserve of his. *But I don't need a challenge,* she told herself. *No time for one — and men clutter up a life so.*

She half closed her eyes. Now, Nels — he didn't make demands, wasn't proprietary, seemed content just being good friends.

And all that could just be a game he's playing, she thought. *Maybe he's just being very, very clever.* . . . As if on cue, the phone rang, and it was Nels.

"Have a good lunch?" he asked. Did she imagine the faint tint of jealousy somewhere at the edge of his voice?

"Delightful," she told him. "Except that Perry had some information about the prop-

erty line between the Campbells and me."
She'd told him about the dumping when
they'd gone out. Nels had laughed sympathetically, saying nobody could do much about
Ernie.

"More problems?"

"I'm afraid so. Apparently there was some
mixup in the figures a long time ago — Perry's
going to check it out."

"Lucas is a good man," Nels said slowly
and deliberately. "In spite of those old rumors.
I wouldn't pay any heed to them."

"Rumors? What rumors?"

"Oh, nothing, really. Just some vague stories about troubles back in St. Louis. He was
pretty strung out when he moved back to
Piney Ridge, but I don't know any details."

Don't know or won't tell, Lauren thought.

"Sleep well, beautiful," Nels said. "I'll call
you later this week."

She realized after she hung up that Nels
hadn't told her his reason for calling, but an
uneasy suspicion teased at her mind: Did Nels
want to cast a shadow of doubt on Perry's
character? But why? Was he a bit jealous, after
all? Pitfalls and complications.

Slightly perturbed, she turned off the TV
and went to bed.

Thursday morning she awoke with a sense

of delicious anticipation. Customers loved local arts and crafts, and finding her own source of country carvings — well, of course it was that idea that brought about the anticipation, not the idea of spending the day with Perry.

And which Perry would she be seeing today? The reserved attorney who hid behind formal words, or the man with a quixotic sense of humor that surfaced too rarely? What was in his past besides the loss of his wife and overwork — if anything? And shouldn't he be coming out of it by now? Darn Nels, anyway!

She dressed in a faded denim skirt and chambray shirt, slipping her feet into comfortable black moccasins. "Back up in the hills" could mean walking over some rough trails. "No caftan," she said to her reflection, almost giggling.

Charlie was shut in the kitchen and she was ready to go by eight-fifteen. She found herself peeking out through the curtains, anxious for the sound of Perry's car, relieved when he picked her up promptly at eight-thirty.

His eyes swept over her approvingly. "Purtier than a speckled pup," he said, opening the car door for her with an exaggerated flourish.

So it was the relaxed Perry Lucas today, she decided with relief. "I don't believe I've ever been called that before," she said thoughtfully. "Thank you, I think."

"Definitely a compliment," he told her, pulling out onto the road. "You're going to see part of the country you haven't seen before, I expect. Have you seen Big Sinking Creek yet, up along the Old Mine Road? Disappears right into the earth, just like that. Hard on the fish, but the tourists love it."

He talked; she listened. He pointed out landmarks; she played tourist and watched him as well as the scenery. His loose white cotton-knit shirt didn't quite hide the breadth of his shoulders. One lock of dark hair fell across his forehead, breeze-caught. This relaxed Perry Lucas was an attractive man. But then, so was the other one — the secretive one — the one who was a challenge.

He pulled off at last onto a rough rutted lane, slowly edging the car along. An ornate whirligig caught her eye, and she felt her antennae sending out signals. Bright little birds watched them from a rail fence — but no, she realized, they weren't watching. The brightness was paint. They were a beautifully carved wooden flock.

"Eureka!" she said softly. "For bringing me here, I owe you one, Perry Lucas."

"And I'll collect," he promised.

Chapter Four

The weather-beaten cottage had a slightly crooked appearance. Mostly paintless porch posts, leaning imperceptibly southeast, supported swaybacked eaves. Hens scratched in the dirt in front of the steps, on which sat a man who matched his house.

He leaned — also southeasterly — watching Perry and Lauren, and as he watched, his gnarled fingers plied a knife that made chips fly vigorously from a block of pine wood.

"He'll cut a finger off if he doesn't watch it," Lauren commented in a low voice, slowing to look over her shoulder at Perry. "And why does he look so suspicious?"

"Jake hasn't nicked himself in years. He looks suspicious because he's reclusive and you're an outlander. Be patient." The corner of Perry's mouth twitched. This encounter could be fun to watch.

"Good morning," Lauren said pleasantly to Jake.

Jake's grizzled eyebrows crawled up his leathery forehead, his sharp blue eyes appraising her through wire-framed spectacles.

Pppttu-u-u-i! A stream of tobacco juice hit

the dust six inches from her trim moccasins.

"Now, mind your manners, Jake," Perry admonished him. "This is Lauren Byrd, the lady I called you about. Say hello nicely, Jake."

The surprised look that Lauren shot at Perry wasn't hard to read: *He has a phone?*

"Hello nicely, Jake," the rawboned apparition drawled with a hint of a smile. He even rose from the step, juggled his knife momentarily, and held out a hand to Lauren with a suddenly shy look. "Just practicin'," he told her.

"Spitting or whittling?" she asked with a smile that Perry thought should charm the socks off Jake MacNab — if he had any on.

"You like whittlin's, do you?"

"Better than spittlin's," Lauren assured him. "Though you do a darned good job of both." This earned her, finally, a real grin from the old man. Perry relaxed. She'd made a good impression.

"You really think there's brainless fools around who'd pay good money for this stuff?" Jake asked her.

She nodded encouragingly. He shook his head. She nodded again. Perry stifled a chuckle.

"Well, then, okay. Some of it's out here, 'course, but come on in the house if you want

— there's lots more. Time waster, 'tis, since Annie Lou passed away and I give up farming."

He started toward the dilapidated front door, then turned back suddenly to stare at Lauren. She took a quick step sideways, apparently trying to remove her moccasins from the line of possible fire, and brushed against Perry. He put an arm lightly, protectively, across her shoulders; perhaps she wasn't quite as self-assured as she seemed. They stood like that for a moment, close, while Jake stared appraisingly at Lauren and the chickens bickered and cackled and a locust started his raspy song. . . .

" 'Course, we'll have to come to terms," Jake said shrewdly. "Don't come 'round here thinkin' to take advantage of an old man."

"Wouldn't dream of it," she said cheerfully and marched briskly forward up the steps. Perry was left with an empty arm and a strangely empty feeling. "You'll find me fair, Mr. MacNab."

So do I, Perry thought a little dolefully and followed the two of them into the dusty interior of the cabin.

Shelves, bookcases, crates, and corners were filled with carvings of infinite variety. A dun-colored old hound lay motionless under an ancient table, looking like a product of Jake's knife. Only a listless thump of his tail betrayed life.

Lauren stood motionless, seeming to search for words; Perry could swear she was almost vibrating. "Well, Jake MacNab," she said at last, "you're darned good at your whittlin'."

He grinned with pleasure and began to talk volubly. He and Lauren discussed, compared, and bargained like two old cronies. Perry half listened, occasionally picking up a painted carved bird or an oil-finished bear or turtle.

A small shelf held a group of figures, roughly carved and wonderfully caricaturelike in detail. Perry picked one up and turned it to the light to study the face.

He put it down abruptly with a sense of shock. There it was again — that grin, those narrowed eyes, the crooked nose, even the cap pulled low over the forehead. The face that gave him sleeping and waking nightmares, the man whose bones lay moldering somewhere along — or in — the Mississippi. Something inside Perry froze, and he straightened and turned away. How could he have felt that opening flower of warmth toward Lauren Byrd when inside him was so much winter?

"And what did you find there?" Lauren said just behind his right shoulder. "Oh — what wonderful little people!" She scooped up several of them, including the one Perry had just put back, and studied them with pleasure. "These, too, if you can part with them," she said to Jake.

"*No!*" Perry exclaimed sharply. He tried to control his voice, smiling weakly. "Homely things, don't you think? Not the sort of things you'd want, really —"

"They're *exactly* the sort of thing I want. Look at the character, the detail. People will love them."

"I don't." He shrugged. "But it's your business —"

"It certainly is," she told him, frowning, obviously resenting his interference. "Consignment, then," she said firmly, turning to Jake. "I'm sure they'll sell well, and I'll take *all* of the little people, please." She shot a look at Perry, who tried hard to look neutral and knew he wasn't succeeding.

He watched her work out details with Jake. A sun ray threw a warm glint from her neat, dark ponytail, and a hint of sorrow he didn't want to analyze mingled with the chill inside him. Jake and Lauren finished their bargaining, boxed the carvings together, good friends now.

"See you again, Missy Byrd," Jake said as they made their way, laden, to the car. "Soon, and with greenbacks, I hope. Bring her back again soon, you hear, Lucas?"

"She can find her own way now," Perry muttered. He helped her stow the box in the trunk, not looking at her, knowing he was being rude but not able to stop himself. She watched him from the corner of her eye, brows drawn together.

In the car, she fastened her seat belt, pulling herself as close to the window as possible. "All set?" he asked in a failed attempt at lightness; he could hear the flat chill in his voice.

She nodded, still watching him. Her antennae had quivered correctly where the carvings were concerned, but she was picking up something else now. Why had he reacted so negatively to the little figures? She hadn't said or done anything to bring this on, had she? His change of mood was puzzling and unsettling.

And, after all, she *did* know what appealed to customers. She tried to squelch the edge of resentment, not too successfully.

"Thank you for introducing me to Jake MacNab," she told him with an attempt at a friendly smile that he didn't even see, since he wouldn't look directly at her. "He's quite a character."

"He is," Perry said, eyes fixed on the road. "You're welcome," he added almost as an afterthought. But he didn't smile.

Lauren sighed. Apparently Jake MacNab

wasn't the only one who was something of a character. They didn't speak much on the trip back to town. She tried to keep her mind on pleasant things, like the lovely scenery and the newspaper-wrapped treasures tucked in the trunk of the car. . . .

My feelings aren't hurt, she told herself firmly. *I should not feel angry just because Perry expressed an opinion. My ego is not bruised. So what if this man has a touch of frostbite in his psyche? I don't care.* But it was rather sad, and she did care.

When he deposited her and her box of treasures at her door, she tried again. "Coffee?" she offered. "As a thank-you?"

"Sorry. I have several things to do. Glad it all worked out. I'll, uh, be in touch." And he turned, abrupt, and strode back to his car.

She watched him drive off, shaking her head lightly. Finally, frowning, she unlocked her front door and turned to pick up the boxes of carvings.

It caught her eye then. She hadn't seen it before, the small flat box sitting to the left of the door. She deposited the carvings inside the door and turned to get the smaller box.

She could smell it even as she picked it up — the heavenly aroma of brownies. Had Lily Mae been by? Though she didn't drive her rackety old coupé any oftener than she had to. Well, she'd call and ask and thank her. But first, price and find perfect places for Jake's work, have a bite of lunch, and hope for a busy, profitable afternoon.

"No, 'twasn't me," Lily Mae said when Lauren phoned her an hour later. "Someone else bringing you goodies, I guess. Secret pals, maybe? Just enjoy 'em, honey." Her voice turned slyly inquisitive. "Where were you off to, anyway?"

"Oh. Perry Lucas told me about an interesting" — Lauren paused and chuckled — "gentleman out near Indian Lake who carves. We went out to see him — strange man, but a darned good carver. Jake MacNab's his name. Know him?"

"Can't say I do. Knew some MacNabs over in Twin Rocks once — probably same tribe. They were a strange bunch too."

"The woods, Lily Mae, seem to be full of odd characters. Mostly men. Though, I guess," she added, trying to be fair, "that was true back in California too. They were probably just odd in a different way."

"Probably. Lauren? You sound prickly as a bramble bush."

And that was probably Perry's fault, Lauren thought — Perry with his friendliness that flashed on and off like a faulty neon sign.

"Sorry, but . . . well. Even Pops is kind of a character, Lily Mae. Ernie Campbell's a troublemaker, and Dutch and Harry are — eccentric, at least, and Jake MacNab *spits,* and Perry Lucas can't make up his mind whether to be charming or chilling."

"Spits," Lily Mae said consideringly. "Some of them do, I guess, but don't mind Perry, now. Remember, he was awful cut up when his wife died. I've known him from a tadpole — he's a good boy. Maybe if you just cheered him up a smidgen —"

"Kiss a tadpole and turn loose a prince? I don't think so, Lily Mae." The memory of her phone conversation with Nels wisped back across her mind; the little niggling questions he'd planted surfaced. "Lily Mae, did you ever hear of any trouble Perry might have been in back in St. Louis?"

"Trouble?" Lily Mae sounded surprised. "No, child. He was just surrounded *by* trouble. What made you ask that?"

"Just something someone said. Probably meant nothing."

"Nothing at all. Don't fret about it. Why don't you just call up Nels and tell him to take you out for a nice, relaxing ride on the lake?" Lily Mae advised. "And come on by soon, if you can, so I can measure you for your new tent, promise?"

Lauren promised, put down the phone, and stared thoughtfully at the box of brownies. Charlie sat close beside her, thumping his tail on the floor gently to remind her that he adored brownies. Now, who. . . .

As Lily Mae had said, she'd probably find out eventually. In the meantime she shouldn't let them get stale, should she? Charlie woofed and grinned in complete agreement with her thought.

Fine gray mists of rain blanketed the hills for the next few days — not great weather for fishing and boating, but nice for shops. Lauren sold two of Jake MacNab's carvings and a good number of items from her stock.

Time for Dutch and Harry to come by again, she thought. And she should go see Pops, talk him into doing some small paintings that would fit into the little empty corners of customers' homes or suitcases. And she'd promised Lily Mae she'd come by.

She'd had no more trouble with Ernie Campbell and wondered whether she should go over and try to have a rational conversation with him — if that was possible — or whether she should work through Perry Lucas on that score. Yet she hesitated to contact Perry. He made her feel uneasy. She didn't need his moodiness, though she did need his help. It was frustrating. Maybe she'd feel better about it if she asked him to bill her for his time. That would put their relationship on a formal, perhaps more acceptable level.

Relationship! She shook her head and smiled.

All those things that needed attention — and the shop was more confining than she'd expected. No time to go "gallivanting," as Lily Mae would say, let alone refinish or restore. Maybe she should see about getting some help. . . .

That evening Glory arrived on her doorstep.

When the front doorbell chimed, Lauren's first thought was that it was a browser ignoring the Closed sign. Her second thought, opening the door, was that perhaps it was Girl Scout cookie time, though the child standing there wasn't in uniform.

Her third thought was that the Walt Disney version of Tinkerbelle had come to life and dressed herself in jeans and crop top to blend with the local scenery. None of those thoughts was correct, as it turned out.

"Hello, ma'am. I'm Glory Mitchell, and I thought maybe you could use some help around here this summer, and I sure wouldn't charge much, but you'd be surprised how much I can do." The words were strung together and spoken quickly, as though re-hearsed many times before Lauren opened the door.

"Oh, my!" Lauren managed, completely at a loss. "Well, I —"

"I'm stronger and older and smarter than you probably think, and I sure could use a job ma'am, so could we talk about it, please?"

"Just how old are you, Glory Mitchell?" Lauren asked gently. The child looked no more than fourteen. "And what makes you think you're qualified to work in an antiques shop?"

The girl breathed deeply and relaxed visibly, now that she was sure she had Lauren's attention. "I'm seventeen. I'll be a senior this year, and I get all — well, almost all — A's. I worked at Logan's Drugstore last summer, so I'm used to working with all kinds of people — even tourists and outlanders." She blushed rosily and looked up through her long pale lashes. "Sorry," she said, in shy acknowledgement that Lauren was an outlander.

She waited for a moment, twisting her hands together nervously. When Lauren didn't answer immediately, Glory added, "I'm right good at dusting and polishing and sweeping floors —"

"That does it, Glory Mitchell," Lauren answered at last, chuckling. "You're hired. Not full time, just a few hours a week, all right? Starting tomorrow morning at ten?"

She watched the elated girl almost skip down the front walk and hoped she hadn't made a mistake. She could almost see magic Tinkerbelle dust sparkling in the air around Glory Mitchell.

The next morning Lauren knew she had made absolutely no mistake at all. Glory was bright, enthusiastic, delightful.

"I'm good at totin' up figures, too, if you need any of that," Glory offered tentatively. "I'd like to study up to be a CPA someday, maybe." She put down the brass candleholder she'd been polishing and looked at Lauren. "And I make good coffee, and I can help you move furniture and all kinds of things."

"Whoa," Lauren said, laughing. "A factotum at slave wages —"

"That's right," Glory said agreeably, as if she knew exactly what Lauren meant. And she probably did, too, Lauren thought.

"Okay," Lauren said. "Let's have coffee and brownies and work out hours for next week, then." She removed the foil from the stoneware platter she'd put the brownies on. "You like brownies? These are special — left on my doorstep three days ago, and they still taste fresh-baked."

"Umm, my favorite," Glory said appreciatively. "They're good. My mama's recipe."

Lauren blinked. "Glory, are you the one who brought these?"

Glory's eyes were wide and innocent. "Not me, ma'am," she said. "I just meant my mama has this same recipe."

Of course. That's all she meant. So who did bring the brownies? The puzzle, one of a long list of puzzles, remained.

"As long as we're going to be working together, Glory," she said after a moment, "why don't you just call me Lauren? 'Ma'am' makes me feel so elderly and proper."

"And you're surely not that, ma'am. I mean Lauren." Glory grinned mischievously, and Lauren started to ask just what might be improper about her, but the jangle of the phone stopped her.

The slightly high-pitched, nonstop assault on her eardrums when she answered made her hold the phone away from her ear.

"Hi there, Miss Byrd. Checking in — open now, are you? Selling good? Got some things you'd be interested in, and we're hittin' a couple of farm sales tomorrow. Comin' through Piney Ridge in a few days. Anything in particular you want? Shall we stop? There's a big auction in St. Louis next week, and we're headin' there next, so if there's anything you want — Oh, this is Harry Johnson. I didn't say, did I?"

"No need to," she told the ebullient picker. "Listen, I —"

But Harry, true to form, was *not* listening. "Shoulda known you'd know. Sharp gal, Miss Byrd. Hey, we got a pine table on the truck you'd love, and a bedside stand, and some kitchen stuff — What's that, Dutch? Oh, Dutch says hi."

"Hi to Dutch," Lauren managed to say rather breathlessly.

"Hi back, she says, Dutch. So do you want us to stop by? Can't stand here passin' the time of day forever, you know. This is a long-distance call and it costs money."

"Right," Lauren said, taking a deep breath, determined to finish a sentence. "Yes, the shop is open, business is good, and I'd like to see you. I have a list — spatterware, yellowware —"

"Sure, got some of those. Anything else? Maybe something we can watch for in St. Louis?"

Lauren closed her eyes and tried to concentrate. And from nowhere — well, perhaps it was the reference to St. Louis — came a vivid vision of Perry Lucas and his steamboats.

"Harry," she said, opening her eyes again so that she couldn't see Perry's face quite so clearly, "I have a customer who collects steamboat memorabilia, so watch for that, and please stop by as soon as you get to Piney Ridge. I'll make up a list."

"You know we'll do right by you, Miss Byrd. Pleasure to do business with you. Dutch and I were saying that just the other day, weren't we, Dutch? See you soon."

He ended the conversation as abruptly as he'd begun it, and Lauren hung up feeling as bemused and amused as she always did after talking to Harry. Dutch probably hadn't contributed many words to the alleged conversation about doing business with her; he was as taciturn as Harry was talkative.

Glory was back to buffing candlesticks to a mellow glow. "Hmph," she said, watching Lauren. "Funny, the kind of junk people buy. If folks were smart, they wouldn't throw anything out. Spatterware? Like your coffeepot, that old speckledy kitchen stuff? My grandma has a cupboard full of it."

"Glory Mitchell," Lauren told her, "if your grandma would like to trade some of that old stuff for some nice new stainless kitchenware, I'd certainly like to talk to her. And I think your education in the antiques business is just beginning."

Perry leaned back in his chair, flexing tight muscles. Paperwork. Mounds of it littered his desk and spilled from folders and made him bleary-eyed.

Odd — he'd thought coming back to Piney Ridge might mean slowing down, even vegetating. At the time, that idea had seemed almost soothing. But it hadn't happened that way. There was little pressure, but he was drowning in detail work. . . .

The showers had passed on, but the humidity seemed a heavy weight across his shoulders. He tensed and relaxed them once again, but knew that part of the tension was not in his muscles but in his mind.

Part of it was Lauren Byrd's fault, he thought, trying to shift the blame to something outside himself. Yet — should the word be "fault" or "effect"? She'd awakened a part of him that he'd been content to let slumber since Caroline had died.

That very fact brought tension and stress, and he just didn't feel comfortable with tension and stress. He wasn't sure he could deal with them. After all, did they sometimes cause short circuits in the mind? Breakdowns? Even violence?

He'd have to be careful. But he'd promised he'd try to reason with Ernie, and he hadn't done it yet. He sighed and reached for the phone, resigned. Perhaps he could take up jogging as a stress reliever. . . .

"Oh, Perry, it's good to hear from you?" Lou Campbell's voice was slightly uncertain, as always. "Yes, Ernie's here — do you want to talk to him?"

"I'd rather talk to him in person. There are some records I want to go over with him, if he's available."

"Now?" Lou asked. "Well, yes, of course. I'll put the coffeepot on?"

"Sounds good. Tell him it's about the property line between your place and Country Blues. See you in about twenty minutes."

He heard a sharp intake of breath on the other end of the line and hung up quickly. Lou was about to ask another question, and he thought he was probably better equipped to deal with Ernie's cantankerousness than with Lou's uncertainties.

If only he'd taken another route that day, or tweaked the wheel more to the left, or come along five minutes later, he wouldn't be in the middle of all this now. If, if. He gathered up the old records. The whole mess was weighted in Ernie's favor, and he'd just have to hope he could work out a compromise. And if he couldn't, he'd still have to go back and deal with Lauren. He flexed his shoulders against the stubborn tension, but it didn't do any good.

Chapter Five

A twitching curtain in a front window of the Campbells' house told Perry he was being watched for. He just hoped he could catch Ernie in one of his rare "reasonable" moods.

There was about as much chance of that as having a nice cup of tea with a grizzly bear, Perry reflected. Still, there'd been times in the past when he'd caught a hint of teddy behind the grizzly. . . .

Parking the car and heading toward the Campbells' front porch, he glanced toward Country Blues. The lots were wide and wooded, and only a glimpse of Lauren's house shone clean and fresh in the afternoon sun. She'd done a good job of renovating — you'd think Ernie would be thankful for that. But there was only so much logic one could expect from a grizzly bear.

It was Ernie who opened the door. "Well, well, Perry Mason himself," he said with a touch of friendly sarcasm. "Not out chasing ambulances today? What brings you to see an upstanding, law-abiding man like me, anyway?"

A wraith of a woman with an overall faded

look appeared behind Ernie. "Ernie?" she said. "Now, Ernie, let the poor man in the door. Come to the kitchen and have some coffee, Perry?"

"We'll prop our elbows and have a proper talk," Ernie said. "If he's got anything proper to talk about. Only one thing I can think of that'd bring you here." He gave Perry a knowing look.

They filed past the overstuffed, antimacassared 1930s furniture, through the small dining room, into the outdated but spotless kitchen. "And what's that one thing?" Perry asked, smiling his thanks at Lou for the steaming cup of coffee.

"That hippie next door and her parking lot that's slopped over onto *my* land," Ernie said smugly. "Might put a fence right across it. Block her driveway, partway, it would —"

"Now, Ernie," Lou interposed, but he went right on.

"And keep all her weird druggie friends and her uppity customers out of my sight," Ernie concluded.

Perry leaned back in his chair and looked levelly at Ernie. "Lauren Byrd may be from California, but that doesn't make her a hippie. Anyway, there aren't many of them left anymore, are there? And some of her 'uppity' customers are people you've known all your life, Ernie. Like me."

Ernie snorted. "Mebbe. But I've seen her wandering around over there, wearing funny clothes sometimes, like some fortune-teller or gypsy or something. Peculiar, she is. Her dog barks, too, whenever I'm near that fence of hers."

"Now, Ernie," Lou managed. "The dog isn't that noisy, and she's covered up decently in those long dresses, and some of them are awful pretty." Lou looked slightly wistful, and Perry could see Lauren all too clearly in her caftanned glory. She must have several of them — decently covered, Lou said. But still, they managed to seem disturbingly sensuous. . . .

"Heathen," Ernie said flatly. "And that *is* my land, right?"

This was the touchy part. "Maybe. Yes and no."

"Typical lawyer's answer."

"Her deed clearly shows her ownership of it, Ernie."

"Ha! Her deed's wrong. Long time ago that land was mine —"

"I found those records too, Ernie," Perry told him softly. "And it was even before your time, and you should have said something about it long before this. Strewing garbage on the parking lot certainly won't settle the matter."

"Now, who says I did that?" Ernie blustered, his ruddy face reddening even more. "Who says? I'll sue her if I have to!"

"Now, Ernie," Lou tried.

This was the time to play his trump card — mention the one thing Ernie might understand clearly, first try.

"It would cost a lot to sue, Ernie. A lot of money and a lot of court time — for a case that I can tell you, as an attorney, might not go all your way." Perry put on his best courtroom face, gazing seriously at Ernie. "Are you prepared for that?"

"You're on her side, that's what," Ernie grumbled, but Perry could see the wheels in Ernie's mind creaking slowly into motion. "I've seen you over there. You're being seduced into sin, that's what's happening."

"Ernie!" Lou exclaimed reproachfully.

Ernie's comment made Perry shift uncomfortably in his chair. "Well, Ernie?" he asked, trying to keep his courtroom face straight. "Maybe a little negotiating is in order?"

"I'll think about it. But I wish that woman hadn't moved to town. Why'd she come *here?* She's a bother, that's what she is."

Perry didn't have an answer to the question and almost agreed with the statements for personal reasons. So he thanked Lou for the coffee, told Ernie to do some serious thinking, and retreated, wondering once again how he'd gotten so involved.

Friday afternoon was hot, heavy, humid, and — it seemed to Lauren — endless.

That morning Dutch and Harry had stopped by, and she'd picked up enough odds and ends from them to "freshen up" her stock. Restless, she moved things around to highlight the new items, a trick she'd learned from Auntie Nell. A slight change of location made both old and new items move better, and she had to evaluate them and inventory them — with a mind that felt like Jell-O that had been left sitting in the sun too long.

It was a relief to put the Closed sign up at six. She walked past the phone, hesitated, and then called Glory. Would Glory like to come over after dinner and see how Lauren coded and priced? Glory would.

She freshened Charlie's water. He'd wisely slept through most of the heat of the day in the coolest part of the kitchen. Now she could shower, slip into a cool caftan, make a salad and a barrel of iced tea. . . .

Twenty minutes later, enclosed casually in her lightweight silver-blue caftan and a faint scent of lemon verbena soap, she began to feel like a human being again. She twisted her hair above her head with Auntie Nell's ivory combs and smiled at herself in the mirror. Now, if she just worked this right, she could sit at the table and drink iced tea, supervising while Glory cleaned up new stock and placed prices and coding in the books. Bless Glory.

She'd barely finished salad and muffins when the blessing arrived at her back door, an energetic pixie in shorts and camp shirt.

"Oh, yes, Lauren ma'am, thank you," Glory said to the offer of iced tea. She hadn't yet quite dropped the "ma'am" but Lauren thought she was making progress.

"I'll bring my books into the kitchen," Lauren said. "There's not enough room for both of us in the office."

The "office" was once a small kitchen porch, long ago enclosed. There was room for a desk, filing cabinets, one chair, and even Charlie, if he curled up tightly and didn't snore too loudly.

Glory caught on quickly to Lauren's procedures. "Card catalog of items and customers," she said gravely when Lauren had explained, "and ledgers and reference books. That makes sense, Lauren ma'am. Lauren. Maybe, though —"

She was interrupted by a friendly woof from Charlie and the sound of footsteps on the back porch. "Anybody home?" Pops's voice rumbled from the dusk outside the door. "Interrupting something, am I? I can come back another time."

But of course that wouldn't do. He had to come in and have iced tea — and an effusive welcome from Charlie — and explain that he kind of "snuck up" because he had something to bring Lauren. And sure now, he knew Glory.

"Worked at Logan's last summer, didn't you?" he asked, beaming at her. "One of the Mitchells. Glad Lauren's got a little help around here." He turned to Lauren and thrust a bulky brown paper parcel at her. "Here. Four little pictures, framed in that old barnwood I picked up last summer. My, don't you look pretty this evening!"

Lauren planted a kiss on Pops's cheek — making him grin almost bashfully — and exclaimed over the paintings. They were vividly done and just what she needed, and she told him so.

"Just something else to inventory, I reckon," he said with a touch of pride in his voice, taking a tall glass of iced tea from Glory. "Thank you, child." The words seemed to take in both Lauren and Glory. "Now, I don't want to be in the way. I'll just settle over here in the corner in the rocking chair and watch and listen, if that's all right. Sure got a lot of books there, seems like."

"Mmm . . . maybe someday I'll computerize all this, but I grew up on my aunt's methods of record keeping, and she wouldn't have touched a computer with an insulated ten-foot pole."

Glory was riffling through the pages of one of the reference books and squeaking disbelievingly at some of the prices. Lauren laughed and switched the girl to one of the ledgers instead. She wasn't three minutes into an explanation of taxes, coding, and sales records when she was interrupted once again by footsteps on the back porch.

This time there was just a brief knock before the door opened and a cheerful "Hey, it looks like a party!" preceded Nels Hawke into the room. He stood just inside, broad shoulders seeming to dominate the kitchen. "You look beautifully cool — or is that coolly beautiful?" he said to Lauren. "Hi, Pops. And let's see — you're a Mitchell, aren't you?" he asked, looking at Glory. "Helping out?"

"Yes," Lauren answered for the girl. "I was going to show her the books — I thought. I suppose you might as well have some iced tea as long as you're here, Nels." She was feeling helplessly outnumbered; this was turning into a social gathering.

"I've had warmer welcomes from my ice maker, but thanks, I suppose I might as well as long as I'm here." He was mimicking her, and she felt a little abashed. "I'd hoped to talk you into a breezy drive along the lake-shore — wrong evening?"

"Thanks, Nels. It was a nice thought. But I'd planned to show Glory how I keep the records."

"Good thought," Pops rumbled sleepily from his chair.

"Great idea," Nels said. "I'll watch. You don't mind?"

Charlie whined, twitched, and closed his eyes, Glory looked expectantly at Lauren, and — why, Lauren wondered, was she not surprised? — another knock came at the back door.

"Hope I'm not interrupting anything," Perry Lucas said through the screen door.

"Come in, Perry, and have some iced tea," Lauren said with a sigh of resignation. She might as well turn on the porch light. A still, rosy twilight was fading toward darkness, and if half the county was headed for Country Blues, she'd better light their way.

Perry stopped just inside the room, looking around. "Oh — hello, everybody. Sorry, Lauren, I didn't realize you had company. Should I come back some other time?"

"Probably," Nels said a little too quickly. "She seems to be pretty busy this evening."

He flashed a patently phony smile at Perry, and Lauren felt a prickle of resentment at his rudeness.

Was Nels jealous? Or did he just dislike Perry? Either way, it was *her* house, *her* kitchen.

"Of *course* you're welcome to stay, Perry," she said more warmly than she'd intended. "I was going to show Glory a few things about the record keeping, but that can wait."

"Record keeping," Perry repeated with a touch of incredulity, looking at the disarray on the table. "I see."

The rocking chair quit creaking, and Pops sat very still, watching. He managed, slightly amused, to say something about Lauren having her own way of doing things at the same time that Glory chirped happily that she was sure she'd learn it all easily.

Lauren fished out the last of her ice cubes and handed Perry a frosty glass of iced tea. "Sugar's on the table there somewhere," she told him. "If you can find it."

"I don't use it," he said with a slight smile, "which may be just as well." The shadow of a smile stiffened in place as he sat down across from Nels. "Hello, Hawke. Resort business good?"

"Good enough. Not so busy that I can't get loose now and then for a little fun." He looked over at Lauren with something that came close to being a leer, and she yearned to shake him.

There *was* jealousy there, and she hadn't done a thing to bring it about. Had she?

The two men eyed each other warily when Pops spoke up, his gentle voice easing the tangle of innuendo that hovered in the air like cobwebs. "Well, honey, I'm glad you liked the paintings," he said, getting up and ambling across the room to put his glass in the sink. "It's time for me to get home. And I know you wanted to get some work done."

Charlie whined his come-back whine at Pops but was ignored. Pops was watching Lauren and the two men at the table assessingly as he walked toward the back door. "You do look awful pretty tonight, child," he told Lauren. "Be good, hear?" His mouth was twitching a little at the corners as he left.

Lauren took a deep breath. Would Nels and Perry follow Pops's lead and let her get on with her evening's work? It didn't look much like it. And why was she sensing hidden meanings in just about every word that was said? Her nerves must be on edge. . . .

And they didn't smooth down when she became aware of the intensity of the look in Perry's eyes. "Pops was right," Perry told her. The coolness of his voice contrasted sharply with the warmth in his eyes. "You look lovely this evening."

"Oh, she always does," said the almost-forgotten Glory, who'd been studying a price guide with absorption. "I like those whatchamacallits — caftans?"

Nels nodded absently, tinkling the ice around in his now-empty glass. Lauren didn't offer to refill it for him. "I suppose," he said reluctantly, "I should be going too." Lauren smiled and didn't try to stop him. "Rain check on that ride?" he asked with a conspiratorial smile.

"Maybe." She walked to the door with him, still very aware of Perry's eyes. "Thanks for the offer, Nels."

Now, she thought, turning back to the room, if *this* one would just leave, she could get back to business. "More iced tea?" she asked brightly before she could stop herself. That was *not* the way to get him to leave.

"Thanks, but no. Actually, I just stopped by to tell you I'd talked to Ernie, and I think he'll eventually come to an amicable agreement and avoid litigation." He was talking and looking like an attorney again. "Just be patient."

"Thank you," she told him. "I do appreciate your help."

"It was a pleasure." He got to his feet, looking as if it hadn't been much of a pleasure, but then. . . . "These things can usually be worked out to everyone's satisfaction."

She walked close behind him toward the back door, and when he turned unexpectedly, there was a near collision. "Sorry," they both mumbled at the same time, stepping apart quickly.

Perry looked at her, at Glory, at the littered table, and then, with apparent interest, at the kitchen faucet. "You know," he told her, "you could probably computerize all this and find it much easier to manage your records. I had an extremely efficient system back in St. Louis, and it helped a great deal."

"I don't care to, thank you," she answered rather stiffly.

"I'm setting up a small system for my office here. Really, computers aren't that intimidating. You have to be organized to run an efficient business. I'd be glad to help you get started."

"Thank you, no." She almost snapped the words, then hesitated, trying to soften her tone. Did he have to poke that handsomely modeled nose into her business?

"Just trying to help," he said easily. "Sometimes people seem to be a little afraid of computers."

Lauren's hands clenched, and she spoke

sharply. "I *choose* not to computerize. I am not afraid of them. I have an MSCS and had a company that developed advanced flow cytometry instruments and scientific information-processing systems —" She stopped, trying to relax. This was ridiculous. "Anyway," she added lamely, "I just don't want one. Okay?"

"Okay." Perry looked slightly stunned. "Sorry. Anyway, I guess it's your business."

"It was, and it is," she told him and watched him walk from the warm pool of porchlight into the darkness of the parking lot. She should have kept her mouth closed. Though he'd asked for it. . . .

"Lordy, Lauren," came an awed voice from behind her. "What was that you just said, anyway?"

"Nothing important, I guess." She turned back to the kitchen. "We still have a little time before you have to scoot back home. Let's just go back over some of the main points. . . ."

Later, putting away ledgers and thinking back, Lauren wondered just what the important things were.

The expression on Perry's face when she'd told him she had a degree in computer science was marvelous, though she wished she hadn't done it. She'd planned to be quiet about her background, once she was settled here. It all seemed long ago and far away, anyway, as if she had been another person.

Trouble is, she thought, *I actually was another person, only I don't know who. And who am I now?* Pulling the deep file-cabinet drawer out to stack the folders, she wondered if she would ever know. It was doubtful.

Frowning, she edged loose the big envelope that was wedged at the back of the drawer. What on earth? She unwound the string that held it closed and remembered.

She'd picked it up during Dutch and Harry's first visit — a large collection of paper collectibles: a 1903 calendar, valentines, an assortment of Tuck postcards . . . and a menu. A bill of fare from the passenger packet M.S. *Sweet Lorena,* showing the dining room; an elegant and ornate menu, featuring food enough to sink the ship and all aboard her.

And of course she had an eager buyer for it.

She sat back in her chair and took the ivory combs from her hair, shaking the heavy dark fall out around her shoulders. She chewed on her lower lip and thought about how accidents, coincidences, and just plain old Fate seemed to be bringing Perry Lucas into her life in so many ways. But Auntie Nell had always said that coincidences weren't coincidences at all; they were part of a Larger Plan about which people knew little and could do less.

Lauren had never been completely convinced, but it was something intriguing to think about. She yawned, slammed the drawer shut impatiently, and went up to bed, determined not to think about it at all.

Perry signed the last of the letters Millie Worley had typed for him and handed them back to her with a smile. "Thanks, Millie. Couldn't get along without you, could I?"

"Oh, yes, probably," she demurred, looking pleased. "But I'm glad for a morning's work now and then, and I'm sure I can type a little faster than you can."

"True," he said. "But, Millie, are you going to object when I get the word processor set up? I mean, is it going to be a problem for you?"

"I may be getting on a little, but I'm not too old to learn something new." She sniffed and turned the corners of her mouth down. "I have nothing against using computers. I can learn."

"Of course you can," he assured her. "But some people don't seem to like them, for some reason." The vision of Lauren in her caftan, fire in her eyes and determination — no, stubbornness — in the tilt of her chin came back to him with astonishing clarity. She really did have such lovely eyes. He wished he could quit visualizing them — and her whole lovely self — quite so clearly.

"Well, it's no problem for me," Millie broke in on his wandering thoughts. "I'll take these letters right to the post office on my way home, all right? See you in a couple of days."

He heard the door close softly behind Millie, half heard her car pull away from the house. But his mind was three and a half miles away, back in the kitchen at Country Blues.

So Lauren had a master's degree in computer science. And what in the heck was cytometry, and what was she doing in a backwater like Piney Ridge, selling antiques, if she'd had her own development company? It didn't make sense. And why should he be stewing about all this when it wasn't any of his concern?

"It's just that inquiring minds want to know," he told the small quartz clock on his desk, aloud but very softly. Another question crowded into that inquiring mind: What part did Nelson Hawke play in Lauren's life? That wasn't his concern, either.

Resolutely he tried to turn his thoughts from Lauren Byrd and concentrate on the complexities of liability laws for a client with a boat-rental operation at Lindsay Cove. He heard a car pull up, thought absently that Millie might have forgotten something, and didn't even look up when he heard footsteps on the porch.

But Millie wouldn't knock, and this person was knocking — odd — most people knew how he operated and just walked into the house as if it were a store. After all, the frosted glass in the front door, with his name stenciled in Steamboat Gothic letters, looked official and businesslike. Probably someone new in the area.

He sighed and put his books aside, stifled the impulse to just yell "Come in!" and went to answer the door properly.

"Yes?" he said pleasantly as he swung the door open with a professional smile — to gaze unexpectedly, and with a jolt of pure pleasure, into the very eyes that had that distressing tendency to haunt him.

Chapter Six

Lauren hadn't really slept very well, after all.

Her determination not to think too deeply about Perry and coincidences hadn't worked. She'd been glad to see him the night before, irritated with him for no really valid reason when he left. *Look,* said a traitorous subconscious voice, *you find him attractive. That's all right. Enjoy it.* Obviously, her subconscious was mocking her reluctance to think about him.

Waking too early, fuzzy-minded, she sat groggily at the kitchen table, drinking coffee and studying the cover of the *Sweet Lorena*'s menu as if it might tell her what to do next. It didn't.

Should she call him about it? Or take it over to him? She *had* been rather sharp with him, and maybe she should apologize; he was just trying to be helpful, even if he did sound condescending. Or was that impression just a knee-jerk reaction to any shaking of the defenses she'd built up, her determined independence?

Wonder where his office is? the small voice deep inside prodded. She found herself checking the town's slim telephone directory — just out of curiosity, of course.

And so, just after eleven, she stood knocking somewhat hesitantly at his ornate front door, almost hoping no one would answer.

But he did. "Hello," he said very softly, his eyes friendly and warm. Eyes that took in, quickly, the menu in her hand and then seemed to assess with approval her beige linen slacks and silky print shirt.

It was a look that made a strange glow travel across her neck, up into her cheeks and forehead. "Good morning," she managed, hoping that the glow wasn't obvious. On the drive over, she had made up her mind that she would *not* apologize for being so defensive the night before. If anything, it was all his fault for offering unwelcome suggestions on how she should run her business. She had nothing to apologize for.

"I came over to say I'm sorry if I seemed edgy last night," she heard herself saying to her horror. "That is, I mean — I didn't mean — well, anyway, I thought I'd bring this by." She clamped her jaw shut and held up the menu.

He wasn't looking at the menu. He was still looking into her eyes, and the glow just wouldn't go away.

"Don't apologize. I was probably getting

pushy." The smile in his eyes deepened and lifted the corners of his mouth to form pleasant creases in his cheeks. She swallowed hard. Why did he have to be so attractive? And why couldn't she tear her eyes away from his face?

"I said I owed you for taking me up to meet Jake MacNab." She held out the menu with a hand that was surprisingly steady.

He finally seemed to take it in. "You're fantastic," he said, taking it from her and looking even more pleased. Of course he was referring to the discovery of the menu, wasn't he? She wasn't sure. And he was asking her to come in, and she was murmuring something polite and probably inane and following him into the house.

". . . the rest of the collection," he was saying, and she gave herself a mental shake. "My office is through here — come in, sit down. I have coffee made. . . ." He turned the menu over, studied the cover, looking like a small boy with a special new comic book. "Maybe this sounds trite," he said, "but you shouldn't have, yet I'm awfully glad you did. Thank you."

She relaxed slightly. That undefinable tension she'd felt between them at the front door had ebbed somewhat, though it still rippled under the surface and between their words.

He poured out the coffee and settled her

in one of the captain's chairs, and she relaxed still further. He obviously took great pride in his collection, speaking of his acquisitions in a way that was somehow touching, as a man might speak of an adored family. The collection *was* impressive.

"You really do love steamboating, don't you?"

"With a romantic passion." She smiled at his choice of words. "Oh, I know about the toughness and inherent tragedies of the old-time river traffic, but still. . . ." His voice trailed off momentarily. "I spent summers working on the river when I was in law school and read *Life on the Mississippi* a dozen times. That's a first edition of it, there on the bookshelves."

She looked at the spine of the book and, on the shelf above, at the picture she had given him of Mark Twain. Next to that —

"Your wife was beautiful," she said softly.

A hint of old sorrows returned to his eyes, and his voice changed subtly. "Yes, she was beautiful. She died when a tornado hit her parents' farm in Illinois. Did you know that?"

"I think Pops told me . . . it must have been awful for you."

"Yes. Sometimes it seems like yesterday; sometimes it seems like another life." The haunted look had come back. He stared at his hands for a moment, then looked up at her with a faint smile. "Guess we both ended up escaping from the city."

"From the city — and maybe from memories." Her voice had a little catch in it. "My Auntie Nell died just before I left, and I had no other relatives. I think I had a small identity crisis after she died. Ridiculous, isn't it?"

"Not at all," he answered quickly. Then, curiously, "You mean you had no other relatives? No one to lean on?"

"I never knew who my father was, and my mother died when I was very young — the term 'flower child' always reminds me of her. I didn't know her family, and neither did Auntie Nell — she wasn't my real aunt, you see. She sort of adopted me."

"Still, you had a good business."

"Yes." She put the coffee cup carefully on the edge of the desk. "It was successful and profitable and not enough." She looked down at her hand, the hand that had put the coffee cup on the desk. It was now covered with a strong, long-fingered hand that looked as if it could manage a giant steamboat wheel quite well. It certainly seemed to be steering her heartbeats into a series of flip-flops.

He settled back into his own chair somewhat abruptly, withdrawing his own hand and intertwining the fingers of both hands firmly and quickly in an obvious attempt at control.

Yet his low chuckle seemed normal enough. "Poor Lauren," he said. "Yet, having too few relatives might be better than having too many — I seem to be related to whole populations up and down the Mississippi and in Missouri. I've heard there's a strain of Cherokee in Oklahoma with the name of Lucas — those old-time fur traders led active lives. I've always been flooded with aunts and uncles and cousins not far enough removed."

He fell silent for a brief moment and then stood up. "Let me show you something. My hall mirror is from an elegant excursion packet." He was back to being the avid collector. "Out on the back porch there's a great old brass and iron bell, and a three-belled whistle that would wake up the whole county if I fired it up. Want to see them?"

"Of course," she told him, and a second later stood beside him in front of an incredibly rococo gilt mirror. Their images smiled back at them only slightly distorted by the inevitable aging of the glass; it wouldn't have taken much imagination to see them both in the elegant costumery of the 1870s. He put his arm lightly across her shoulders and nodded, as if pleased with the handsome picture they made.

She blinked at their reflections, and then, in a conscious escape from the mirrored past, up at the real Perry Lucas.

His eyebrows drew together, and the familiar shadow dropped about him momentarily. But she was only vaguely aware of it, because her eyes closed of their own accord when his other arm went round her and he pulled her to him and kissed her. Gently, caressingly, as if her lips were rose petals he was afraid to bruise, as if he were holding back with almost superhuman effort.

She realized, fighting the waves of pure longing that engulfed her, that her own arms were around his neck. She disentangled them and managed, breathless, to stand back. It was one of the most difficult things she had ever done.

"I didn't mean to do that," he said tensely. "I'm sorry."

"I'm not." She could have bitten her tongue, but it was too late; it was said. And he'd turned away from her now, looking off into the recesses of the long hall.

"No, Lauren, it shouldn't have happened." The cool, proper attorney was returning, and she felt cold, pushed away, rebuked for her warmth and response. A little chill of hurt anger scrabbled at her throat, and she couldn't speak. "I appreciate your bringing the menu to me," he was saying. "The kiss was — was a thank-you."

"Oh, yes, of course it was. Thank you for your thank-you."

"Don't be angry. You don't quite underst—"

"No, I guess I don't, quite. I must hurry if I want to get a bite of lunch before the shop opens, Perry. Glad you liked the menu, at least. I'll see you." She retreated, low heels clicking on the bare oak floor and the door slamming angrily behind her.

What on earth was the matter with the man, anyway? Someday she'd face him down, fix him with her best cold stare, and ask him exactly that.

No, she wouldn't. She didn't care to care that much. But the broken shards of her shattered ego were jabbing her in unexpected places, and the van tires squealed in protest as she roared around the corner, away from that impossible man.

Charlie, sensing her mood, politely declined to come back into the house with her when she got back to Country Blues. Flopped at a distance with his head on his paws, he watched reproachfully as she dug for her house keys.

She almost apologized to him, but that was

silly. Standing with key in hand at last, she closed her eyes, took a deep breath, and tried to will away her anger. It didn't work very well.

And when she opened her eyes and looked down, there it was — another small box, similar to the one the brownies had come in. It was a wonder Charlie hadn't tried to open it for her. "Good boy," she said and picked it up. Charlie didn't move, though he thumped his tail once. He obviously still didn't trust her mood.

She let herself in, put shoulder bag, keys, and box on the table, and eased off the lid. Gingersnaps, richly redolent of autumn kitchens. . . . She ate three and felt a small amount of her hurt and anger drain away, so she ate two more. Only the ringing of the phone kept her from turning into the Cookie Monster.

"You won't believe — just will — not — believe — what great stuff we picked up in St. Louis!" crowed the voice on the other end. "It was the estate of a ve-e-ery wealthy old geezer, 'twas, with town houses and country houses and probably houses he didn't talk about in polite company. The international dealers got the best stuff before the auction, but still — Wait'll you *see!*"

"Wonderful, Harry. What kind of —"

"Have to get up early to beat out some of

these dealers, you do. Lots of bidding, but we got some books for a buddy of ours in Columbia, and Oriental stuff for another buddy in Springfield, and then we're stopping by your place. Hi from Dutch."

"Hi back," she said automatically. "When will —"

"Should be there tomorrow afternoon or evening. Have your checkbook ready and chill some beer for us, okay? Bonus, like, 'cause it all costs money, you know, including the phone call. See you." Abruptly, he was gone. Lauren put the phone down and went back to the cookies, turning one over and over as if looking for a signature. She sat down at the table, thoughtful.

Where on earth *had* the cookies come from?

Had Harry remembered her request for steamboat memorabilia?

And if he had, would she get in touch with Perry?

Staring glumly out the window, she ate the cookie.

"I thought I'd better get here early, since Dutch and Harry will be here later today." Lauren's voice was muffled through the half-finished caftan she was sliding over her head.

"Watch out for the pins," Lily Mae said. "They will, will they? Humph. And Harry told you to have cold beer ready, right? Old freeloader. That looks real nice, honey. When I put the finish trim on, it'll be fit for a queen. Stand still now."

"It's beautiful," Lauren said truthfully, peering into Lily Mae's mirror. She didn't feel at all like a patchwork quilt, as she'd feared she might. "Ouch!"

"Told you to look out for the pins. There, now. Real fetching, it is — I wasn't always a wrinkled old prune, you know. I know what kind of clothes make a woman feel good, what makes the men around them feel good too."

Lauren shook her head and smiled. "You're incorrigible."

"Guess so, if you say so. How's Nels? How's Perry? You still being standoffish?"

Lauren squelched a tiny flare of anger. She wasn't sure whether it was directed at Lily Mae's unquenchable romantic curiosity or Perry's apparently very quenchable romantic impulses. She couldn't be angry at Lily Mae, after all, so that left. . . .

"I've told you and told you," Lauren said teasingly. "I didn't move to Piney Ridge to find a man. I want to find *me*, and I'm not interested in involvements. I just want to make a new life, set up my own nest —" She could believe it while she was saying it; up until recently it had been the honest truth.

"Yup. Told you so. Nesting instincts — you're admitting it yourself. Let's have some tea."

There was something soft, and yet strong, and certainly totally disruptive about the way Lauren had fit into his arms. Perry stood at the window and looked out with blind, bleak eyes. His sleep had been fitful. He had dreamed of Lauren, of telling her the truth, of being completely honest with her.

And in the dream she had reacted with horror. Retreating from him, wearing a filmy, shimmering caftan, she had screamed "Never, never, never!" and then disappeared in a pinpoint of light.

It was, after all, only a dream. But it had been followed by another — of that face, that leering dirt-streaked face, the struggle, the uncertainty. . . .

At last he called Millie and told her not to come in.

"I haven't been able to start anything today, anyway," he said, trying to sound offhand and cheerful. It didn't ring true.

"You just go off someplace and relax," Millie told him. "You've been looking a little peaked lately, anyway."

"Thanks," he said. That didn't sound like

the right response so he said "Right," and then he gave up and chuckled a little, though there was no humor in him. "I guess I'd better take my vitamins," he told her. "See you Monday or so."

"Going off someplace" sounded like a good idea, so he tried it, but he found he couldn't leave his thoughts and emotions behind. He spent an hour walking aimlessly, broodily, on the grounds of Hahatonka, the looming old ruins of a mansion that stood above the lake. He thought of Lauren. He thought of the past. He tried to think of the future, and that was depressing.

Finally he turned and strode back to the car. He'd call Joe Reilly, back in St. Louis, and talk to him again. He'd go back to the city, if necessary, and check all the files again and track down the truth one way or another.

He'd been told to forget about it and start a new life, and he'd done his best, though it hadn't worked well, and it was working even less well since he'd met Lauren.

He'd find the truth, no matter how much it hurt, and then he could deal with the future. One way or another.

Lauren flipped her sign from Closed to Open, propped the front door invitingly wide, and put baskets of bright dried flowers and an assortment of eye-catching items on the porch.

The roses were blooming again along the repaired fence as if they'd never been nearly uprooted, never had their growth and integrity challenged by a car skidding out of control. She wished she could say the same about herself.

By the time she'd finished lunch, Glory was tripping up the back steps. Her hair had been tortured into an approximation of the serene crown Lauren herself sometimes affected — except Glory's fine blond hair had escaped wispily, helter-skelter.

Lauren secretly felt a little pleased. "Do you want me to brush it in more tightly for you?" she asked, and Glory beamed.

"Thank you, Lauren," Glory said in awe when she'd examined the results in the small mirror by the hall door. "That's surely chick, isn't it?"

Lauren agreed that it was, indeed, chic and had the girl get the ledgers and books from the office. "We'll need every last one of them in the next few days, I expect. Dutch and Harry are bringing in quite a load. Think we can handle it?"

"Oh, yes, Lauren, I know we can." Glory suddenly looked a little shy. "I had an idea, you know? About the coding. I thought and thought about it last night."

Lauren checked the six-packs that were chilling in the fridge, offered Glory cookies and root beer — and learned that no, Glory knew nothing about the cookies — and settled down at the table to listen to Glory's ideas.

And marveled. Glory had, indeed, come up with a twist to the coding procedure that would simplify cataloging. "So who needs a computer?" Glory asked triumphantly when she'd explained.

So there, too, Perry Lucas, Lauren thought and grinned at her young helper. "Not us," she said. "No way."

It was just shortly after one when they heard Dutch and Harry's truck grinding into her parking lot — the small vintage moving van always sounded terminally asthmatic, yet managed to cough its way over country roads and wheeze into cow pastures where sales were being held.

Lauren watched Dutch and Harry seem to fall out of the doors, stretching and stomping off the stress of handling their muddy behemoth. Harry's jaw was moving full speed even as he stretched his thin, wiry arms; Dutch, taciturn as always, stifled a yawn and then caught sight of Lauren and smiled his slow smile.

"Now, now," Harry said, following Dutch's

gaze and seeing Lauren. "Important things first. Dutch and me'll just have a beer, and *then* I'll open the truck. You're gonna like this too — worth waiting for. Come on, Dutch, I got enough dust in my throat to silt up the Missouri."

It wasn't until she'd herded them into the kitchen and popped the tops of a couple of cans of beer that Harry fell silent for a moment, gazing from Lauren to Glory and back again. But it was a very short moment. "Got a helper, have you? Pretty too. 'Course, you're the prettiest dealer I ever had on this route, Lauren Byrd, ain't she, Dutch? But then Dutch wouldn't know. He's just a greenhorn kid in this business."

The solid, gray-haired Dutch hardly fit the description. Lauren knew he'd retired from the railroad several years back and somehow hitched up with the voluble Harry, a forty-year veteran of the trade. So he was still learning — but a greenhorn *kid?* No.

"Have some potato chips," she offered and looked longingly and meaningfully out the window toward the truck.

Harry chuckled. "Sure, thanks. Just let me finish this beer, and we'll go open up the truck. Lucky, we were, with this lot. Lots of wholesalers there bidding — why, we hardly got our bid confirmed before these guys in business suits came storming in, creating a fuss about what had already been sold."

"Sharks," Dutch contributed succinctly, looking wise.

An hour and a beer later, they were still unloading. Glory was an enthusiastic helper; Lauren was happily sorting through crates and mentally rearranging the stock. This should see her well into the tourist season. There were some fine things. . . .

"This here, now," Harry said, patting the top of a small steamer trunk he'd just eased from the truck. "This and that big trunk over there, and a couple of old Gladstones — good condition, got some linens and stuff in them, pretty salable. And in this crate here" — he picked it up with care and put it down on the parking lot with an absurdly pleased look — "this I had to get, just for you, Laurie. Ain't cheap, I'll warn you, but just what you asked for."

Lauren looked curiously at the crate, then up at Harry. What had she asked for?

"Steamboat model," he said reverently. "All handmade, nigh on to seventy-five years ago." He slid the top of the wooden crate off, eyes bright with pleasure. "Said you had a buyer for old steamboat stuff, didn't you? Couldn't ask for anything to warm the heart of a steamboat collector more than this would, now, could you?"

"No, Harry," Lauren said in a small voice, staring at the beautifully detailed model that was coming into view. "Nothing. Nothing at all. Thank you." She could imagine the look that would come into Perry's eyes when he saw this, and for a moment she felt ridiculously jealous of a seventy-five-year-old steamboat model.

The phone call came about midafternoon.

"What do you mean, the papers are missing?"

"They just are. They're gone. Look, we tried —"

"Try harder. What about the safe-deposit vault?"

"Jacoby's son checked it out; we saw to that. Nothing there. They should have been, but maybe the old guy took them out —"

"If you value your life, you'd better find them. What would the old man have done with them?"

"How would I know? That stupid coronary took him off so fast. Who knows how an old kook's mind works? We talked to the housekeeper, though. She was there when he died."

"What would she know about it?"

"Maybe nothing. We just tried to be nice, jog her memory, like. And he did say something interesting just before he died. Something about skeletons in the closet. We checked them, of course, but not fast enough, I guess."

"No skeletons, you idiot? What did you expect?"

"Just shut up and listen, will you? There'd been a bunch of old stuff in the closet, it seems, but it got packed up and sent off to auction the day before we were there."

"Ah. Then you go to the auction and bid high."

"Too late. The auction was going on before we knew."

"Fatheads! Start tracing now — who bought what —"

"We've already done that, boss. Got dealer friends who can tell you lots of things for fifty dollars or so. Coupla pickers named Johnson and Mueller got most of the Jacoby stuff. And listen up. They told somebody they had a real good market for it — including a new dealer down around Piney Ridge."

"Piney Ridge. Piney . . . son of a — All right, I'll call there. And, you two — follow up. Fast."

The line went dead.

Chapter Seven

The price of the steamboat model was rather high. Lauren didn't hesitate, though. As Harry pointed out, she apparently had a ready buyer for it. He'd bid kinda high, he said, but if she didn't want it —

She did, of course. Harry would make his profit; she would make hers. And Perry would be delighted, although a contrary little whim was already wisping through her mind: She just might keep the model for herself.

"We got a load of canning jars for Lily Mae this trip, so we'd better head up there. Cheap, they were. Might trade them for a piece of cherry pie, if she has any made."

Dutch brightened and finished stacking the last boxes for Lauren. "Now?" he asked Harry.

Harry nodded. "I guess. Thanks, Lauren. We'll see you again soon — sell lots, and don't let that steamboat go too cheap."

She picked up the model after they were gone, cradling it in her hands beside the kitchen window. The detail was exquisite. The sun struck tiny highlights from the brass fittings; it glowed with a life of its own.

She wouldn't call Perry. At least not right away. She'd just display it with a Not for Sale sign and enjoy it herself.

Partly, she truly did want to treasure it herself for a while, and she really didn't want to call Perry for any reason at all. She had a slightly bruised ego, after all, if she wanted to be honest about it. She could still feel the sting of rejection when he'd turned from her, stern and cold, after that kiss. . . .

"I'll just put it on that pine step-back cupboard," she said, hardly realizing she was speaking out loud.

"It's Mr. Lucas who collects steamboat things, isn't it?" Glory asked from beside the kitchen sink, where she was washing up some of the new crockery and glass. Lauren jumped; she'd nearly forgotten Glory was there.

"Well, yes. But I'll get in touch with him a little later."

"Nice man, Mr. Lucas." Glory had a shrewdness in her eyes that reminded Lauren of Lily Mae. "You two look nice together, you know that? And I think he likes you."

"Yes, he's nice. Good heavens, Glory, watch what you're doing. Those are valuable R.S. Prussia bowls. I'd better help you before you break something."

Glory looked up in surprise at the edge in

Lauren's voice, then gave her a tiny apologetic smile.

There were times when Lauren wished Glory weren't so quick and observant. . . .

They were busy "settling in" the fresh stock for several days. Glory worked hard, accepting with equanimity Lauren's eventual apology for having snapped at her; she just looked wise and nodded, ironed linens, and rubbed new oil into old finishes.

Customers browsed through, and the stock moved well. There were a couple of offers for the steamboat that almost tempted her — she turned them down and then wondered if that was foolish.

An extremely "chick" woman from the Chicago area examined everything in the shop. She had eyebrows penciled into a permanently inquiring position that was slightly supercilious, and clothes so obviously tailored for the city that Lauren took an immediate and illogical dislike to her. That dislike was tempered somewhat when the woman, with (it turned out) the improbable name of Penelope Peabody, bought three of Pops's smaller paintings.

"And if," Ms. Peabody said, paying cash from an impressively thick stack of hundred-dollar bills, "you should care to send me snapshots of some of Mr. Carmichael's future work, perhaps we could work out satisfactory arrangements for shipping?" Ms. Peabody left her business card: interiors and custom designs.

Well. Wouldn't Pops be pleased!

"We'll put off going through the trunk and that box of paper items," Lauren told Glory. "Dutch and Harry probably checked it pretty carefully for anything really valuable."

"The trunk itself would sell pretty quick, fixed up a tad," Glory said, running fingers over the curve of the domed top.

"You're learning fast," Lauren told her with a laugh. They transferred the papers to a sturdy cardboard box and stowed it, for the time being, in the pantry. And then, when the quiet little man who collected Confederate money and documents came in, she wished she'd started the sorting out a bit sooner.

"I have nothing in stock like that right now — that I know of, anyway. There's a new shipment that hasn't been completely checked out — still in boxes back there." She gestured toward the rear of the house. He offered, a little too eagerly, to help her sort and then gave her his number and said he'd be back. She doubted that; Be-Backs seldom showed up again.

During a lull she found her long-handled

sable watercolor brush and meticulously dusted the steamship model. She hated to part with it . . . and maybe she wouldn't. Maybe she'd just keep it.

It was a day later before Lieutenant Joseph Patrick Reilly returned Perry's call. And when he did, his voice had a note of friendly exasperation. "No, Perry, nothing new has ever come up on that. You were supposed to be forgetting all about it."

"I've tried." Perry made a face, tapping his pencil on the desk, wishing he could make Reilly see how serious this was to him. "Between you and that darned stress counselor who needed a shrink, I've heard 'forget it' over and over. I can't."

"Should have tried a different counselor. Because no one was reported missing, we never found a thing about the guy."

"He could have turned up downriver."

"We've been all over that possibility, and you know it. No, Perry. You'd been working too hard, and that night you'd been drinking too hard, and maybe you got into a donnybrook with some old drifter — who knows? But look, friend, I've known you for a good part of your life, and I know you're not homicidal."

"I wish I knew that for sure. Maybe I'm

just paranoid, but underneath it bugs me that I don't quite know what I'd be capable of under the wrong kind of stress. I just need to *know*."

"What's bringing it up now, anyway? There's been a lot of water under the bridge since then — Sorry, shouldn't have put it quite that way, maybe. But by now it should be behind you."

"It is — right behind me, with a hand on my shoulder. If it was real — well, I don't want it to recur. Yeah, I know I drive you nuts. Look, maybe I'll see you next week. I'm coming back to town to talk to some people, try to convince myself. . . ."

"Well, you're a bit crazy, but you're nice crazy. Come by and see me, then."

Perry sat staring into space for several minutes after he hung up, vaguely aware of a fly buzzing against the window, of the soft whir of his ceiling fan. *What's bringing it up now, anyway?*

It was a good question, one he was reluctant to face: He was afraid he was on the brink of falling in love again, something he never thought he'd do. He turned to look at Caroline's picture. She smiled at him, and he could almost hear her voice telling him to get on with his life.

"I'll try," he promised. He straightened his

shoulders — and the papers on his desk — and even tried to whistle a few bars of "Meet Me in St. Louis," but the whistle trailed off. . . .

There were too many unanswered questions. Lauren was intelligent and sensitive. Maybe he could just tell her about it, but he still recalled that dream, when he'd told her and she'd run from him in horror. She wouldn't really do that, would she?

Eventually he might have to share the uncertainty with her, but for now, he had to try again to find the truth. And stay away from Lauren until he'd exhausted all the possibilities.

Keeping his distance from her turned out to be more difficult in practice than in theory. After all, Piney Ridge was a small town. He shouldn't have been surprised the next morning when, at the only local food market of any size, he rounded the corner of an aisle and ran, almost literally, into Lauren.

She seemed caught off guard, a little uncertain. There was a moment of uncomfortable silence, then tentative smiles. "Hello," she said. "Nice morning, isn't it?"

"Hello," he answered. "Yes. That is, if you like rain."

The corners of her mouth curved up enchantingly. "I do." Her voice was as gently firm as if she were reciting wedding vows.

He felt slightly rattled. That was the only explanation he could give for his next words — that he was rattled. "I just stopped by to get some cornflakes," he said, "and why don't we go across the street and have a cup of coffee together? There's something I wanted to talk to you about."

Her smile faded, and for an awful moment he both feared and hoped that she'd say no. She looked puzzled, and why not? If he couldn't understand himself, how could he expect *her* to?

"Well." She looked at her watch. "I have a little time before the shop opens. Shall I meet you in ten minutes?"

"Good," he said, absently picking up a jar of instant coffee — which he detested — and heading with abrupt haste for the checkout. She must think him mad. Maybe she was right. *Because,* he thought as he paid for his purchases, *why did I do that? Why couldn't I just comment on the weather and then leave?*

He tried to be rational. He wanted to let her know that he'd be out of town for a week, that was all, so that if she needed him, she'd know about it — she was sort of a client, after all.

"Mr. Lucas, you forgot your change!" the

clerk called. Red-faced, he collected it and hurried through the fine, wind-whipped droplets of rain to Jenny's Café. A table for two in the window was free. Good. No, he told Liz, the waitress, he'd wait just a bit before he ordered; he was being joined by a friend.

The "friend" came out of the market just a few minutes later, hesitated, then headed for the parking lot. She wasn't coming, after all, he thought, his heart sinking. It rose again when he saw her stow her groceries in the van, say something to Charlie, and then head toward Jenny's. Charlie. He was always with her. Darned nuisance of a dog.

Her hair was loose today, swirling around her shoulders, catching raindrops that clung like jewels. Odd, even in jeans and windbreaker, she managed to look like a goddess. . . .

He took a deep breath and tried to regain control of his thoughts as she spotted him and slipped into the chair opposite him. Liz was there before either of them could speak, with two cups of coffee and a big smile for Perry. Her smile didn't include Lauren. "Thank you," Lauren said, half to him and half to Liz's retreating back. She looked thoughtful, somewhat sad.

"Something wrong?" He suddenly felt absurdly protective.

"No, not really. Just —" She hesitated. "Sometimes I wonder if I'll ever be accepted here." She looked him straight in the eye. "People in Piney Ridge can be rather un-friendly at times. Unpredictable."

Is she talking about me? he thought. *What do I say?* "It'll pass," he heard himself state levelly. "You'll see."

"Of course. And I mustn't forget I have some good friends."

"That's right." He smiled and hoped his smile was reassuring. "And the others will warm up eventually. People who've been born here, lived here forever, tend to be clannish."

"And I don't belong to a clan. I'm just a strange antiques dealer from California, where palms and swimming pools grow and the ground shakes." She was almost smiling now. "Dutch and Harry stopped by with some won-derful things from an auction," she said.

"Anything I can't live without?" His voice sounded too cheerful in his own ears. His smile probably looked fake too. More like a leer, probably.

But she wasn't looking directly at him. "There are a lot of things that one can manage to live without," she answered softly at last, staring into her coffee cup.

How should he interpret *that?* He was con-sidering several possibilities when she looked up at him again. "You said you had something you wanted to tell me," she reminded him.

"Oh. That. Yes." For a moment he fumbled — what was that rational reason? "Yes. I just wanted to let you know I'll be gone for several days, maybe a week. Some — unfinished business. Unexpected complications I hadn't anticipated previously —" There, he was doing it again — talking like a frock-coated jurist, and for the life of him he couldn't stop himself. "In any case, if Ernie Campbell should attempt to contact you, it might be advisable to tell him to defer any decision on the property dispute until I return. . . ."

She had a very peculiar look on her face, as if she didn't know whether to laugh at him or throw her coffee at him. "I am such a nuisance, aren't I?" she asked wryly. "Thank you for the information. I really have to get back to the shop. If Ernie Campbell sets foot on my land while you're gone, I promise not to talk to him at all. I shall simply get out my little Winchester varmint rifle and blow his trespassing toes off."

She stood up, donning her windbreaker and easing her heavy hair out from under the collar with a gesture that was almost queenly. He rose, too, knowing exactly what a "blithering idiot" must feel like. She laid a dollar bill on the table, saying something about it covering her share, and turned from him with chin high. He could do nothing but stare after her retreating back with a feeling of utter helplessness.

"Don't give up on me, Lauren," he mumbled after her, but she gave no sign that she'd heard him.

Why on earth did she find that crazy pedantic way of talking that Perry sometimes used so doggoned appealing? There was something endearing about it, and yet she hated it — because it was frustrating, a curtain that fell every time she was just beginning to enjoy the show. Was he hiding his real feelings, or did he just not have any real feelings?

Darn him, anyway! "Get out of the way, you dummy," she grumbled at Charlie, plopping her bag of groceries onto the counter. Charlie looked hurt and retreated under the table.

"Who needs it?" she asked rhetorically. "Not me." Charlie twitched an ear and closed his eyes, sighing. "There are many things one can really live without," she added in unconscious repetition of her earlier words to Perry. But Charlie was no longer listening, and perhaps she wasn't, either.

When the phone rang at eight-thirty that evening, she almost didn't hear it. Head in one of the old trunks and ankle-deep in musty, dusty papers, she was a century away from Country Blues. Breathless, she caught the phone just before the answering machine took care of it for her.

"You sound out of breath, love. Did I take you away from something important?"

She sneezed, almost resenting the twentieth-century intrusion on her nineteenth-century thoughts. Almost resenting Nels's easy use of the breezily meaningless word "love." "Sorry," she sniffed. "Dust — an occupational hazard. Just going through a trunkful of papers and odds and ends that Harry and Dutch brought by. Nothing very exciting, I'm afraid."

"I have an idea that might make it more exciting. I can bring a bottle of wine over, and we can sort papers together. Read hundred-year-old love letters and dream of days of yore —"

Lauren laughed. "Sorry, Nels. I haven't seen a love letter in the lot yet, and I doubt if yore was all it's cracked up to be. I'm just going to finish up the boxes in the pantry and one in the cellar and call it a day — and you sound as if you'd be more of a distraction than a help."

"That's what you drive me to," he said with cheerful resignation. "Distraction. Let me whisk you away from all that dust Saturday night. We could drive to Indian Grove for dinner, drive beside the lake in the moonlight, stop at the Cottonwood Club. Please say yes. I need an escape from the Nest."

There was an almost plaintive note under the humor. She couldn't think of a good reason to say no, and Nels's easy good nature might divert her mind from thoughts of Perry. For a while, at least — and so she said yes.

And for a while, at least, Saturday evening went as she'd hoped. She dressed in style in cream silk and even did her nails — something that was low on her list of priorities these days, thanks to such things as paint thinners and steel wool and sandpaper. And Nels's appraisal of her told her he approved.

Perry probably wouldn't have even noticed — *Stop that!* she told herself severely. *You're not to think of him tonight.*

It was a forty-five-minute drive to Indian Grove, and the evening was romantically soft and misty. But she wasn't going to think of romance, either. This was just an evening out with a good friend who didn't expect much of her except her friendship. Did he? His attitude was so different from Perry's, though they were both sometimes difficult to read.

She reminded herself sharply that she wasn't going to think about Perry. Her nerve endings were beginning to feel sandpapery.

"Something wrong, Lauren?" Nels asked as they pulled into the restaurant parking lot. "Are you with me? You're so quiet."

"Just . . . enjoying the scenery. Sorry," she said. This just wouldn't do, and she made a small face at herself and then gave Nels the smile that used to totally disarm CEOs who had to be convinced that a young woman could be both intelligent and attractive. He seemed reassured; she wasn't sure *she* was.

But dinner was good; the wine was excellent; they danced well together. She heard someone comment in a low voice that they were a nice-looking couple. Would they have said that if she'd been dancing with Perry? Darn, she was doing it again!

Maybe it was the wine, or maybe it was the strawberry-lemon soufflé — but back at the table she found herself falling into silence again. Lonely somehow, even with Nels. She watched a family group at the next table, and thoughts that often haunted her came unbidden to deepen her mood.

Families. . . . Who had her mother been, really? And what had happened to her father? Who was she? That was something she'd been trying to find out all of her life. She'd loved Auntie Nell deeply, but there were still the unanswered questions. Most of the time, just being herself — just being Lauren Byrd — was enough. But sometimes the questions came back. . . .

"Something wrong? Something I said?" Nels's tanned hand was on top of hers, bringing her back to the present with a jolt. "Maybe you've been working too hard. Maybe you need a little more romance and moonlight and me in your life."

He was smiling lightly at her, but she caught a serious undertone to his words. She decided to ignore it. "I apologize, Nels — my mind's wandering. I promise to be good for the rest of the evening."

"Oh, darn, must you? That's not what I had in mind."

Oh, darn, indeed! "Let's dance," she suggested, and they did. She concentrated on lightness, charm — and distance. She told him about Ms. Penelope Peabody and Pops's growing success. She talked of Glory's invaluable help, and Dutch and Harry's peculiarities. . . .

"They're originals, all right. Bring anything interesting this trip? Like those love letters among the papers? Or was it all just old throwaway stuff?"

"I rarely throw anything away," she told him severely. "One man's junk is another's treasure, as the saying goes. There were scrapbooks, some good floral prints, old photos — nothing that you'd care about at all."

"I guess I just don't appreciate hundred-year-old junk — sorry, Lauren, *antiques*. But maybe you could teach me? Maybe I could learn to care — and perhaps teach you a few things in return."

She laughed uneasily and changed the subject. There was little doubt: Nels was getting serious. *Bite your tongue, watch your step, and keep it cool,* she instructed herself. It might be her imagination, after all, or a typical macho-male jealousy of her new friendship with Perry. She could handle it.

But Nels watched her rather strangely, slightly subdued — for Nels — and on the way back to Piney Ridge he seemed to be deep in thought. She wondered, feeling edgy, what he was thinking about.

He didn't leave her in suspense long. Easing his Jag purringly along the side of Country Blues at last, he turned to her almost before he'd come to a stop.

"Lauren —" Did she detect a note of uncertainty in his voice? "I don't want to make you uncomfortable." He reached over and put his hand over hers, making her more uncomfortable than ever. She resisted the impulse to snatch it away. He took a deep breath and spoke again, sounding more like the old Nels.

"I'd just like to spend more time with you. Get to know you better. . . ."

"Do we know each other at all?" she asked before she could stop herself and immediately felt slightly ashamed. "Sorry, Nels. I don't mean to hurt your feelings. I do like you."

"Like is such a nice, neutral word, isn't it?"

"Can we leave it like that for now? It's a truthful word."

He thought for a moment and then looked at her with an unreadable smile. "Friends?" he asked.

"Friends."

"I'll give you a call, friend." He didn't even try to kiss her good night, and she stood on her back steps, watching the baleful red glow of the taillights disappearing out the drive.

So much for all her great intentions of keeping men out of her life for the time being. Both Nels and Perry were definitely *in* her life — and problematical for such different reasons.

Speaking of friends, for heaven's sake — "Charlie?" she called. She'd left him dozing on the porch, food and water at hand. He was good about staying put, but where was he now? "Charlie!" Maybe she should have shut him in the kitchen. But there. There was a faint answering bark from the direction of the garden shed. Still, in the dim light, she couldn't see him.

Another bark — he was in the shed, the fool dog. How did he manage that? The shed door was closed. Had it been ajar and he'd wandered in and — "I'm coming, Charlie!" she yelled. She picked her way carefully over the uneven ground in her high heels, giving up midway and taking them off.

"One more pair of wrecked panty hose," she grumbled, yanking open the shed door. "Your fault."

The eyes that looked up at her from a lowered head were more than merely apologetic. They were glazed and unfocused, and the dog moved with uncharacteristic hesitation.

"Hey, guy, you okay?" Her anger forgotten, she guided him toward the house. "Let's go in and take a look at you. What's the matter, Charlie?" She fumbled in her small satin envelope purse for the house key, then fumbled again, trying to find the keyhole.

She must have forgotten to set the timer, she thought. The back-porch light should have come on hours ago. And then, with key at the keyhole, she realized that the door itself was slightly ajar.

Chapter Eight

First, a surge of fear-induced adrenaline. Then shaking hands and a pounding heart as the pieces fell into place.

Charlie had been shut in the shed; the timer light was off; the back door was not securely closed. At best, she'd probably been burglarized; at worst, the intruders might still be in the house. Her mind whirled, seeking avenues of action or escape. She steadied herself against the doorframe with a shaking hand and looked down at Charlie.

He sat beside her, looking up. He looked groggy, but he was aware of his surroundings. Logically, if his canine senses felt that someone was in the house, he'd be barking. Instead, he was very quiet, inquisitive rather than alarmed.

Silently, she reached inside the door and flipped on the light switch. The kitchen light flooded the room. It looked reassuringly normal, but she was leery. It took a long moment and much courage to take that small step inside.

Charlie whined and followed her slowly, slinking toward his tennis ball and his favorite spot under the kitchen table.

"No, you don't, you coward," she whispered. "You come with me." He lumbered reluctantly to his feet and came to stand close beside her, almost leaning against her leg.

Nothing seemed to have been disturbed, but then, outside of the small television on the kitchen counter, there wasn't much that would appeal to snatch-and-run specialists.

Her stock, though. The case of antique jewelry on the dining-room sideboard, the R.S. Prussia, the steamboat model — If it were knowledgeable antiques thieves who had broken in. . . .

Lauren stood motionless, listening, and had an eerie feeling that the house listened with her. *Ridiculous!* she thought, but still didn't move a muscle. There was no sound of movement, no creaking of floorboards, no one scrabbling to escape guiltily into the night. The refrigerator motor clicked on. The normality of it made her relax a little.

She picked up the big meat cleaver that hung above the chopping block and started forward. Probably she could never swing it at another human being, but it was protection.

The light in the narrow butler's pantry between kitchen and dining room revealed nothing amiss. She switched on the dining-room light, looking apprehensively toward the pine cupboard that held the steamboat model.

It was there. So were the R.S. Prussia bowls, the baskets, the small case of jewelry. Nothing at all missing or moved. . . .

Relief made her sigh audibly. Still, there was the living room. Charlie at her heels, she moved quietly to the arched doorway between the dining and living rooms and turned on another light. Nothing was wrong, nothing missing. "Okay," she said to Charlie in a voice that shook a little with a combination of fear and relief. "Let's make some tea."

It seemed a soothing thing to do, and besides, she desperately needed to sit down. Charlie, looking relieved, went back under the table with his tennis ball. He seemed almost as normal as the house now. "But what were you doing in the shed?" she asked him while she waited for the kettle to boil. "Why wasn't the back door closed? Why didn't the light come on?"

He had no answers.

The whys wouldn't go away. She carried the cup of tea to the table and sat down, staring at the tea bag swimming limply in the steaming water. The night gathered around the house, deep and dark and full of questions. A glance at the timer told her it was set at "off." So perhaps she'd forgotten to turn it on.

Possibly. She doubted it. And Charlie hadn't shut himself in the shed, and he'd acted so peculiar. She got up and checked his food and water bowls. They were empty and told her nothing. She didn't like the direction of her thoughts, but. . . .

Could she have left the back door insecurely closed? Could Glory have come over for some reason? Glory did have a key, and maybe — But that didn't seem like Glory.

Lauren took the lukewarm tea and limp tea bag to the sink and disposed of both. In the morning she'd check with Glory and she'd look over her stock again, but now it was time to try to get some sleep. If that was possible.

A willing but bewildered Charlie obeyed her order to come upstairs with her. He loved to sleep at the foot of her bed but didn't very often get the chance. It was his gentle snoring that finally, even as the sky lightened, lulled her to sleep.

The insistent ringing of the phone jarred her awake just a few hours later. The sun was already hot and strong through the windows. Charlie's good-natured muzzle was propped inquiringly on the edge of the mattress as she struggled free of sheets and dreams to grab the cursed phone. "Yes?" she managed to squeak.

"That dog of yours," an accusing voice said.

"Barking all night. Some people have no consideration."

She fell back onto the pillows, limp. Ernie Campbell. Not exactly a gentle wake-up call.

"Do something about it," he was saying. "I don't like to complain, but —"

"Oh, yes, you do," she managed to say. "It's your favorite occupation." She sat up, trying to marshal her thoughts. "Barking? Look, he usually doesn't do that. . . ."

Memories of the night before swept back over her, and she came sharply awake. "When?" She had, appropriately enough, almost barked the single word and tried to soften her tone. "I mean, what time did you hear him barking?"

"Most of the evening, from nine till ten or so. Anyway, having fits, he was —"

"Nine until ten isn't all night," she pointed out reasonably. "Sorry, Ernie, I wasn't here. But — well, could someone have been prowling around, do you think? Was it that kind of bark?"

"Chasing a dad-blamed squirrel, more likely. I can call the county dogcatcher, you know, if that mutt's going to be noisy."

Lauren swallowed hard and reached out to lay a protective hand on Charlie's trusting head. "I have reason to think," she said, slowly and distinctly and hoping her words might penetrate Ernie's hard skull, "that someone might have been trying to break in here last night. It sounds as if Charlie were just doing his job."

"Couldn't he just bite them and shut up about it?" There was a little less anger in his voice, though, and that made it easier for her to be conciliatory. After all, hadn't Perry warned her to stay clear of any arguments with Ernie?

Easy for him to say. He didn't live next door to Ernie. "I really am sorry he disturbed you. I'll leave him inside after this when I have to be gone."

"All right. Long as you understand I like peace and quiet."

"I understand," she said levelly. Darned if she was going to apologize again. Putting the phone down, she stared into Charlie's limpid eyes. "Sooo. Who were you barking at, anyway?" she asked but received nothing but a tail wag in reply.

Glory, when she arrived about eleven, wasn't much help, either. No, she hadn't been there the night before. Her eyes reflected alarm. "Gee, Lauren, you could have been hurt!"

"That thought did occur to me," Lauren told her dryly. "But I'm not sure anyone was here. There was a little cash in the desk drawer, and it's still there. It doesn't make sense."

"Maybe you should call the sheriff?" Glory's eyes lit mischievously. "Might make his day — nothing much exciting ever seems to happen around here."

"I hope it doesn't start now," Lauren answered. "Besides, what could I tell him? Nothing's damaged or missing. But how could Charlie shut himself in the shed?"

Glory, shaking her head, went off with the lamb's-wool duster in hand.

An interesting, if improbable, thought crossed Lauren's mind. Could Ernie have shut Charlie in the shed because he was so annoyed by his barking? But there was Charlie's lethargy. . . . Lauren sighed and headed for her small office. There was paperwork to do, and she might as well get at it.

She stopped short in the doorway, staring around the office.

Surely she'd left those manila folders at the left side of her desk. They were in the center now, slightly askew. And one of the file drawers was ajar, jammed by protruding papers. She was sure she hadn't left it that way.

Glory's voice directly behind her made her jump. "Did you start going through those boxes on the shelf in the pantry? 'Cause if you didn't, the box moved itself over about a foot. Sure you don't want to call the sheriff?"

"Maybe I should," Lauren murmured, puzzled and uneasy. "Because someone *has* been here. But why? What did they want?"

The deputy sheriff, a thin young man with hollow cheeks and sharp eyes, asked the same questions when he finally arrived around two P.M. He came to the back door quietly, unobtrusively, which Lauren appreciated. She left Glory in charge of the front with the three customers who'd browsed in.

"No," Lauren said in answer to his questions. "Nothing seems to be missing, but I'm sure someone was here." He looked skeptical. She could understand that.

He said he'd try to keep an eye on the place. Since the county wasn't exactly overstocked with police officers, Lauren could only take the assurances with a grain of salt and thank him for coming. After he left, she checked on Glory. Glory was doing just fine, thank you, Lauren ma'am, having sold a set of mixing bowls and another of Jake MacNab's carvings.

Glory was obviously enjoying herself, so Lauren dragged boxes of papers to the kitchen table and checked over them. She wasn't really familiar enough with the contents to know if anything was missing. It was frustrating.

Maybe she should talk the situation over

with someone levelheaded and discerning, someone who might help her get a new perspective — like Lily Mae. Or Pops. Or Perry.

But Perry was in St. Louis. She stared glumly out at the still summer afternoon, reluctant to admit how melancholy that fact made her. It wasn't logical, and she was always logical.

When the telephone rang, it was the one person she hadn't thought of calling, in spite of her excess of logic.

"Just a — a friendly call, love. To tell you how much I enjoyed your company last night even though I couldn't get you to admit that you're madly in love with me. You are, you know."

He seemed back to normal. "Hi, Nels," she said. "You don't give up easily, do you?"

"Missouri mule," he agreed cheerfully, then turned serious. "I just wanted you to know that I'm sorry if I came on too strong last night, but the truth is, I love your company. It was a great evening. Hope you slept well and had wonderful dreams."

She shuddered a little. As matter-of-factly as possible, she told him about the possible break-in.

"And there was nothing missing," he mused. "You're sure? What could be valuable in those boxes of papers, anyway?"

149

Lauren sighed. "It makes no sense, I know. I've even tried to tell myself it was just my imagination. But someone *was* here."

"It was really incredibly careless of whoever it was to leave things a little messed up. You'd think they'd be neater. Still, I don't like the idea of your having gone into the house, not knowing for sure what was going on."

"I didn't think much of it myself. But everything's okay."

Nels permitted himself a small sympathetic laugh. "Maybe they just weren't antiques fanciers — I can understand that. The nicest thing in your shop is the proprietor, as far as I'm concerned. Look, I don't mean to make light of it. Would it help if I came over and went through some of the boxes with you? Give you a shoulder to cry on, or moral support, or just an ear?"

"Thanks, Nels, but not right now. I'll manage." She was very much afraid that a trickle of sympathy from Nels could turn into a torrent of encroachment that she didn't want to handle. "I'll be in touch," she promised and hung up.

She hoped she hadn't been rude, but her nerves were edgy. Where was all that wonderful peace and serenity she'd come to Piney Ridge to find, anyway? Squeezing her eyes tight shut, she tried to visualize herself as calm, controlled, unruffled. It didn't work well at all. She wasn't any of those things. All right. She'd stay up every night, if necessary, to go through all those things Dutch and Harry had brought — to look for clues.

And she'd call a locksmith to put new locks on the doors. The intruders had managed to get in so easily. She frowned. There hadn't even been any damage to the doorframe. They were apparently well experienced. The thought made her shiver.

A few high-flying clouds and all-pervasive thoughts of Lauren followed Perry all the way to St. Louis. She'd bewitched him — raindrops in her hair, sunlight in her eyes. The tilt of her chin and the delicious softness of her in his arms haunted him. He wished he could think of just about anything else.

But when he tried, he was still haunted — this time by the unpleasant ghosts of the past. He made himself concentrate on the road. After all, exorcising ghosts was the primary reason for this trip. He'd have to come to terms with the past so that he could realize his visions of tomorrow — many tomorrows.

With Lauren. If she'd have him.

He checked in at his motel by three and immediately called Joe Reilly. Sure, Joe would have dinner with him. They could go over the whole thing one more time, though Joe couldn't see what good it would do. Wasn't it bad for the digestion to hash over old nightmares? Well, if that's what Perry wanted.

Obviously old nightmares — especially those that belonged to other people — didn't interfere with Reilly's digestion. He settled his considerable girth back in his chair after polishing off a double order of barbecued ribs and leveled a serious look at Perry. "You've met a girl," he said, looking pleased.

Perry grinned. Nothing much ever got past Joe Reilly. He could read the fine print, the spaces between the lines, and then see behind even that. Which was why he had risen steadily and impressively in the police ranks.

"Not a *girl,* Joe," he corrected. Lauren would hate being called that. "An attractive and intelligent woman."

"Mmm. Okay." Joe made a face. "And you don't know how she'd react if you told her you thought you'd killed someone. Which you didn't — I wish I could get that through your head."

Perry rolled his spoon over and over between his thumb and forefinger. "And I wish I could be as sure as you are."

"When you called today, I checked all the missing-persons records for the past year — two years — again. Four bodies, and none of them fit the description you gave. Why, oh, why" — his deep voice turned plaintive — "don't you just let go?"

"I've tried. Honestly, Joe. But — look, maybe the guy is on a 'missing' list in Memphis. Or Chicago. Or Kansas City."

Joe leaned forward intently. "Perry, I've known you a long time. You're not a violent man, never were. If you decked some old guy, he was probably trying to mug you, and I expect he took off for Dubuque as fast as his drunken legs would carry him."

The familiar chill of desperation spread over Perry's mind and body. "We fought. He went in the river. He didn't come up. Joe, I *killed* someone —" He squeezed his eyes shut, and the distorted face and rheumy eyes he'd seen so many times seemed to appear like an evil genie, blocking out rational thought.

"Joe! I see it now — a gold tooth. He had a gold tooth." The face swam out of focus and faded, and Perry opened his eyes to see Joe shaking his head at him sympathetically.

"Sure. A gold tooth it was. I'll make a note of it. And who was that shrink you were seeing before you left town, Perry?"

Perry stood below the Eads Bridge the next morning and stared downstream toward the Arch, watching the excursion boats, the barges. As always, the sight brought a measure of peace to his mind. He'd like to bring Lauren here, tell her the old stories. . . .

But first there were other things to take care of: a stop at the old city offices to say hello, and a trip along the river to check out every bar between here and Jefferson Barracks. And if his searching turned up nothing, he'd go back to Piney Ridge and explain himself as well as he could to Lauren Byrd and hope that she would understand.

He drank very little these days; he avoided stress; he was dependable, honest, loyal, lonely, and in love. Very much in love. That thought cheered him somehow and may have been part of the reason his ex-cohorts — still slaving midst legalities — told him he looked great. He almost regretted that he was no longer part of this. Seeing his old desk brought a twinge, knowing that he'd had to leave unfinished business. . . .

"Be grateful you're out," Marshall Short told him from behind the desk that had once been Perry's. "Legal loopholes, cons a-conning, apes appealing —"

"And a partridge in a pear tree?" Perry grinned, but quickly fell serious, thinking of the case that had immersed him so completely. "The Clovis case, Marsh — any luck?"

"None. Suspicions but no evidence. The

Feds took it over, you know, and a clever defense team finagled indefinite postponement of what little we had. Your baby, wasn't it?"

"It was. Wish I could have stayed with it."

"Forget it. Crooked financiers with dirty money build clever houses to hide in, you know."

"And innocent investors get hurt," Perry said sadly.

"Go back to the hills and relax, Perry. You'll live longer."

Probably true, but it was a shame they'd never gotten enough on Clovis and his cohorts to prove fraud. . . .

By midafternoon he'd found little bars he couldn't remember ever seeing before, tucked away on side streets near the river. It had to be near the river. And none of the bartenders, bored-looking in the yeasty murk of a summer afternoon, could help him at all. They looked at him curiously and shook their heads when he ordered ginger ale and asked questions about a man he described from his own haunted visions.

No, Perry said, he wasn't a cop. He just wanted to find the guy. He parted with several ten-dollar bills and received only vague shrugs and offhand wishes of good luck, buddy. He finally ordered a beer at the last bar and sat for a long time staring at nothing.

By four he leaned against the big cannon on the bluffs at Jefferson Barracks and decided he would probably never find answers. Best to get on with life, after all. He'd go back to the motel and call Lauren and tell her he missed her.

It turned out that he didn't get a chance at that last part. She sounded truly glad to hear his voice, which was almost surprising, considering he hadn't been very — well, dependable or predictable or loving. Another thing to rectify, he thought with a grin and asked her how things had been going. The answer startled him.

"Someone broke in," he repeated, stunned. "Nothing was taken. You weren't there. You weren't *there?*" A tiny stab of jealousy put an edge on his voice, and he tried to squelch it.

"I was out for dinner with Nels," she told him, and the small stab became a near-mortal wound.

"Oh," he said. "I see." The break-in was the important thing. He'd have to head back immediately so that he could protect her — from break-ins, of course.

"But why would anyone break in and then not take anything? Where was Charlie? And what did Nels do about all this?"

"Nels didn't come into the house with me

156

and didn't find out about it until the next day. Charlie — well. . . ." He listened as she explained, coolly and concisely. He reflected a bit ruefully that it didn't sound as if she needed all that much protection. She'd apparently handled it all very well, calling the sheriff, going over her records for clues.

But it was puzzling. "You think they might have gone through your papers and the things Dutch and Harry brought?" He thought of the wildly haphazard stacks of records and papers he'd seen on her table and repressed a chuckle. Good luck, burglars. "I'll be back in a couple of days — maybe I can help. Maybe you have old photos someone wants to keep a dark secret, or an original manuscript of *The Raven* — something spectacular you didn't even know about."

"Maybe," she said doubtfully. "But I think I'd have spotted something like that by now."

The repressed chuckle refused to be repressed any longer. "I don't know, Lauren. I've seen the way you organize your papers and records — if organize is the right word."

It might be the right word, but it was the wrong thing to say. He knew it as soon as he'd spoken. He could have bitten his tongue. When Lauren said good-bye, there was a polite but distinct note of coolness in her voice.

He sat and stared at the phone after he replaced the receiver. Why did he have to sound so darned smug and superior? He wasn't laughing at her, not really. Or if he was, it was with love. He suspected he was going to have a heck of a time convincing her of that fact. She had little sensitive spots, unexpected vulnerabilities.

That thought led to others, somewhat associated and very pleasant. He leaned back on the hard motel bed with his arms locked behind his head and let his mind drift into the wonderful world of possibilities.

Chapter Nine

Lauren hung up the phone and stared down at Charlie, who was curled up complacently under the table. He stared back, unwinking.

Why am I so touchy, anyway? she asked herself. *I'm taking everything Perry says so personally. . . .*

From far off on the less-traveled paths of her heart and mind, an inner voice told her exactly why, whether she wanted to hear it or not — she wanted Perry to accept her. More, to admire her. To care about her and respect her — in spite of any peculiarities she might have. Not that she could think of any of those, not right offhand.

Because, darn it, she accepted, admired, cared about, and respected him. In spite of any peculiarities he might have. And he did have some. "Oh, yes, he does," she said aloud, and Charlie thumped his tail agreeably.

Yet if she were really honest with herself, maybe it was unfair to think of him as having "peculiarities." It would be more accurate to say that there were things about him that she didn't understand, that were mysterious and as yet unexplained.

If she were *really* honest, she'd have to admit that there was something about him that stirred a primitive longing in her that went far beyond admiration, respect, and simple caring. Though those things were all mixed up in what she felt about him.

All mixed up. That was a pretty apt description of her feelings, at that — a rich stew of wariness, yearnings, and puzzlements, all jumbled confusingly together.

By the time Glory arrived the next morning, she'd had long, dark hours of the night to think — about things, people, problems, peculiarities. And she hadn't come to any conclusions. Not intelligent ones, anyway.

"You know, Glory, I think I'll take Friday morning off. Could you open for me about eleven, if I'm not back? I need a little break."

"Man problems, Lauren?" Glory asked with that understanding look in her eyes that was so unexpectedly adult.

"No, nothing like that." She could see Glory didn't believe her. "I want to go up to Jake MacNab's — we need more of his carvings. And I thought I'd take a picnic and give Charlie a chance to run off some of his excess energy in the hills."

"Oh, yes, he surely does need to do that," Glory agreed, looking down at the motionless, snoozing dog. Then she looked up at Lauren and grinned. "Have fun," she said.

Experimentally, Lauren left Glory alone for almost two hours that afternoon while she herself ran a few errands. Glory handled the customers and the paperwork beautifully. Tinkerbelle was a treasure.

Late in the afternoon she put photos of Pops's work in an envelope addressed to Ms. Penelope Peabody, called Jake MacNab, and felt as if some things, at least, were under control. When Nels called in the early evening, she was able to tell him, without fibbing, that she'd be busy for several days.

She needed to keep Nels at a safe distance. Perry was already at a safe distance, almost too much so, in St. Louis. She could enjoy her picnic and think about . . . things . . . people . . . problem solving. Coolly and objectively and optimistically.

At eight she showered and slipped into the new caftan Lily Mae had made for her, pulled her hair back into a ponytail, and admired her reflection in the mirror. The caftan was charming, and she'd picked up a golden light tan this early summer — along with about five pounds. Her face looked softer, more relaxed. She had been a little too thin, cheeks drawn and eyes shadowed, by the time she'd sold the business and the town house. . . .

You see? she asked herself. *Everything's working out.*

And Friday would be a perfect getaway.

By Friday morning the weather settled into a pattern of cloud-flecked skies, glowing sunlight, and fresh breezes. Lauren awoke with a feeling of anticipation. Going back up into the hills for a few hours struck her as just exactly the right thing to do.

She donned sneakers, jeans, and a comfortable oversized print shirt. After an enormous breakfast she made a picnic lunch of egg-salad sandwiches and Lily Mae's tomatoes, and slipped a couple of doggie treats for Charlie into her picnic basket.

By the time she'd had a second cup of coffee, she'd made a decision. She wouldn't think about problems, peculiarities, or anything at all that might upset the sunshine of this day. She'd go see Jake MacNab, stop for lunch, play with Charlie, just let it all hang out today. No worrywarting. After all, she did enough of that during the long hours of the night, didn't she? Too often.

Charlie apparently picked up some of her thoughts, for he grabbed his tennis ball and raced joyfully toward the van when she picked up her keys.

And she had no trouble finding Jake's cabin

in spite of his very peculiar directions; she remembered some of the turnings from the trip up with Perry. Roads turned into graveled tracks where the trees curved lushly above and creepers swung in the breezes.

Jake heard her coming and was waiting at the bottom of his crooked steps for her, hands on hips and a smile on his face.

He didn't even spit.

He seemed genuinely glad to see her, but then he would, wouldn't he, this time? Because her first words made his eyebrows shoot upward in glee and a wide smile spread over his face.

"Have an envelope for you, Jake. One hundred sixty-three dollars and fifty cents, cash. And a check for seventy-five more."

"Hot darn!" He gave her a cheek-splitting grin. "Who woulda thought it? Come on in, Miz Byrd, I got another boxful for you. I'll make some coffee — mind the dog, now."

There wasn't much to mind. Jake's dog lay like a sack of potatoes on the porch, and when Charlie ran inquisitively up to touch noses, the old tan hound simply opened one eye, blinked, twitched an ear, and went back to sleep. Charlie went to sit, disappointed, beneath the cottonwood tree that looked as if it were propping the house up. Or maybe it was the other way around.

Lauren declined the coffee, though he assured her that it would put hair on her chest. "Thanks, but I really don't have the time. I'm stopping for a picnic on the way back," she told him, taking the box of carvings. "Saw a little dirt road about two miles south of here that looked as if it led up into a meadow."

"Most of those little roads wander up into nothin' at all. Except poison oak and wasps' nests, maybe. Be careful now."

She would, she told him. She called Charlie and waved back at Jake's lanky form, bouncing the van as gently as possible over ruts and bumps and between chickens.

She glanced at her watch. Just a few minutes past eleven. There was plenty of time for picnic and play. No problem.

The beckoning lane was waiting for her. Judging from the looks of the crowding underbrush, it wasn't used much. She eased the van cautiously over the rough tracks. For a moment she thought of abandoning this one — after all, it looked as if the rest of the world had done so some time ago — and trying another.

But then she saw the golden reflections of sunlight on a glade just ahead. Bouncing the van over one last set of ruts, she turned off the ignition. Perfect.

The woods gathered close around a blanket

of flower-sprinkled green grasses. At one side, a strangely humped hill rose stony and vine-covered from the meadow floor with an almost fairy-tale loveliness. The sun felt like a blessing as she unloaded picnic basket and blanket, realizing she was very hungry.

She ate, watching Charlie explore, returning to her frequently with soulful eyes that requested a bite of egg-salad sandwich. He loved egg-salad sandwiches. When he saw that she apparently was going to devour most of the "people food" herself, he stood with nearly the same expression in his eyes, but with the tennis ball in his mouth.

"Who says dogs can't talk?" she asked him, laughing, and spent ten minutes in a game of toss-and-catch.

But then he lost the ball in the long weeds and grasses at the base of the rocky hillside. "Dumb dog," she said and went to help him find it. She found something else instead — something much more interesting than a tennis ball.

Behind heavy shrubbery and a veil of creepers was a small opening, just big enough to let in a ray of sunlight that fell across the rocky floor of the cave beyond.

She stepped inside and felt the cool mustiness envelop her almost at once. Beyond, she could see the fissures in the rock widening into a passageway on the far side of the cave. Just for fun, she shouted "Halloo!" toward the roof of the cavern, chuckling to hear the echoes bouncing around her in a ghostly chorus. Charlie, who had been close at her side, looked up at her in alarm and bolted back out into the sunlight.

"Craven coward!" she shouted after him, and the echo returned. Lauren stood still for a few minutes. The cool dampness crawled up the flesh of her arms and across the back of her neck. Then, tentatively, she went forward to investigate the fissures.

Dark. Very dark, but it seemed to be a passageway. For a moment the conservative part of her mind warned her of bats and rats and other unknown and unknowable creatures of the darkness.

"Charlie?" she called softly, but he sat firm just at the entrance to the cave and refused to come back in. All right. She'd get the flashlight from the van. She'd just check quickly for things like stalactites, stalagmites, mineral deposits — and maybe hidden treasure. Hadn't someone — probably Lily Mae — told her of rumors that Jesse James had hidden some of his stolen riches in the caves of the Ozarks? There was a child in her who yearned to explore a cave and had never had one to explore.

Even with the flashlight to bring the details of the cave into focus, though, Charlie would have nothing to do with it. She called him twice, then decided she'd have to explore by herself. Which was just fine; he had a tendency to run off to do his own investigating and might get lost. He whined anxiously when she stepped into the deep shadows of the fissure — like a worried nanny, she thought. "Stay," she told him — unnecessarily, as he'd obviously decided to do just that. "I'll be back soon."

The passageway was damp, chillier than the entrance cave had been. And narrow and dark. Perhaps she should turn back. But the reassuring beam of the flashlight picked up a crooked vertical shadow on the uneven limestone walls just ahead on her left. Curious, she edged her way toward it, just to see. . . .

The shadow was the entrance to another small cavern. Her light picked up the sparkle of dripstone and calcium deposits that glittered on all sides within. Marveling, picking her way across damp, slippery rock underfoot, she edged closer, to touch, to see.

And then there was another passageway opening at the side of this one — she hesitated for only a few seconds before moving into it. Of course she could find her way back. She hadn't gone far — she'd just take a look and then get back to the sunshine and Charlie.

It was a curving downhill passage, strewn with fallen limestone and curiously dim.

With a chill of fright that shot through her like icy needles, she realized that the dimness was not a mist in the damp, silent reaches of the caves. It was a result of the batteries in her flashlight growing weak.

She turned back, trying to hurry, trying to swallow her panic. Her right foot slipped and twisted painfully beneath her, and she dropped the flashlight and fell to her knees.

Grabbing at the flashlight, she tried to stand. A muscle reaching from her heel into her calf tightened with a fiery stab. *I'll sit still for a few minutes,* she told herself, *and then it will feel better.* She switched off the flashlight to save what little life was left in the batteries and knew, with awful certainty, what the absolute dark of the tomb must be like.

There were very few calls on Perry's answering machine when he got home. He listened to them with half his mind, the other half hopping about like a slightly drunken grasshopper.

Call Lauren — lay it all on the line. She'll understand.

No, don't do it like that. Take it slow. How

do you know she'll understand? How do you know she even cares? And what can you tell her, anyway?

There hadn't been any definite answers this trip, and there might never be, but what if —

The phone rang, and he overrode the answering machine.

"Mr. Lucas? I'm so glad you're home. This is Glory — Glory Mitchell. I just wondered what to do. It just isn't like her —"

"Slow down, Glory. Do about what?"

"She isn't back yet — Lauren isn't. She went up to pick up some stuff from that Jake Whoozit and said she might be a little late getting back. I can handle the shop just fine, Mr. Lucas, but she should have been back two hours ago."

"I'm sure she's fine," he said, but a premonitory chill ran down his spine. "Did you call Jake to see if she's been there?"

"Yessir, I did. He said she had, she left for her picnic, and maybe she just lost track of time, but I'm worried."

"Try to relax, Glory. I'll call Jake, and we'll find her. There's nothing to worry about. You'll be at the shop?"

"Until I know Lauren's all right," she said fervently. "I get feelings about things sometimes, Mr. Lucas, like my grandma does. And

169

I don't like the feelings I got right now."

There was something contagious about Glory's "feelings." That rough, winding road that led to Jake's — Had the van gone off the road? Was Lauren injured, far from help, alone? Of course not. There was a logical explanation.

He called Jake MacNab, but there was no answer. Jake could be outside. Perry let the phone ring on, clenching his teeth and willing Jake to pick it up, but at last he gave up. On impulse he called Lily Mae. No, Lauren hadn't been there. Had he tried Pops? A shadow of worry whispered in Lily Mae's voice.

And Pops hadn't seen her, either. "Want to drive up toward MacNab's place and see if we can spot her?" he asked, his voice a little gruff with puzzlement and concern.

"Where would we start? She could be anywhere." Perry tried hard to be logical. "She'll probably be back any minute, anyway. But I'll try calling Jake again. I'll get back to you."

This time Jake MacNab answered — a laconic, rather surprised "Yeah?" Perry almost smiled. Jake probably didn't get that many phone calls. This made two calls and a visitor, all in one day.

"Yeah, she left about — oh, I'd say eleven

o'clock," Jake said in answer to Perry's first question. "Said she was going to have a picnic lunch. Didn't even have time for a cup of coffee." He sounded aggrieved. "Said she saw a likely turnoff about two miles south of here — Oh, gawd."

The sudden drop in the gravelly voice on the last two words sent a warning shock along Perry's nerve endings. "Gawd," Jake repeated before Perry could say anything. "Culpepper's Bend, that would be. White Dog Cave. Horseradish and tarnation, Perry, that could be trouble. Listen, I know right where that is. You got time to come up and get me? Because if that's where she is, it'll take two of us to bail her out of there. At least. You know how to get hold of the county search-and-rescue unit?"

Time, Lauren thought, was such a relative matter.

That simple, unoriginal thought had never before loomed as such an overwhelming truth. How long had she sat there in chill fear? It seemed forever. She tried the flashlight again. Nothing. She knew the low wail that filled the blackness around her was her own voice, but it made her shiver anyway. . . .

Water dripped somewhere in the distance. *Alone,* she thought, *in a dank, unfamiliar world.*

Not even Charlie. . . . She almost called him, but even if he could hear her, what if he got lost too? She couldn't do that. There must be some way out.

She tried to think, running her hands blindly over the rocks around her. This was the bottom of a slope, wasn't it? She'd come gradually downhill — could she make it back to the top?

Her painful ankle throbbed at the pressure when she tried to stand, and she fell back to her knees. All right, darn it, she'd crawl. At the top maybe she could see some light.

It was even more difficult than she'd anticipated. Hands and knees slid on the damp, slippery rocks. The wet chill soaked right through to her bones. At one point her left hand and supporting arm slid out from under her, throwing her against rough stone.

Struggling back up to her knees, she grasped her arm. Mud? Or blood? It felt like both. She bit her lip and continued inching her way up the slope, only to find more darkness. Total darkness. Was there light anywhere? She stared off in every direction, trying to see something — *anything*.

And for a brief second she thought she did see something, far off down what must be a passage — an animal, a misty, white doglike figure. She called. No reaction. It trotted weightlessly and silently out of sight, evaporating into the blackness of the cave. Lauren put her head down on the cold wet denim that clung damply to her knees and let the hopeless tears take over.

"Pops? Want to help?" Perry had called the older man as soon as he'd finished talking to Jake MacNab. "I'm sure there's no cause for panic, but —"

"Panic, no. Reasonable concern, yes. Now, listen, throw some extra blankets into your trunk and bring a strong torch, rope, a first-aid kit if you don't already have one in your car. Stop at the café and fill a thermos with hot, sweet tea, if you can. And hurry up. I'll be waiting for you on the front porch. I'll call the county emergency crew while you're on your way here."

"Right," Perry said and hung up with a peculiar brew of emotions simmering through his system. Lauren might be perfectly all right — she might even laugh apologetically at their concern.

Though she'd better *not* laugh. He'd be tempted to shake her if she did, after giving them all such a scare. And Jake could find her if she were lost. He knew the place, he said. Even so, Perry thought, he might shake her for being such a fool as to wander off into the caverns all alone.

No, he wouldn't. He'd be too busy holding her, loving her, telling her how much she mattered to him.

Behind these thoughts lay a faint sense of surprise. That hadn't sounded like Pops Carmichael on the phone. He'd lost the easygoing drawl, had barked commands like a general. He was still barking when he sprinted toward Perry's car like a man half his age. "Just called Glory. Lauren hasn't come back. You've got everything? How long does it take to get to MacNab's?"

"Got everything, and about forty-five minutes of driving like a maniac. Fasten your seat belt." He could sound like a general too, if he had to. Pops gave him an approving half smile.

They talked little on the way. The county dispatcher, Pops said disgustedly, didn't seem to be too concerned about getting someone out. She'd said that it was probably a false alarm, but she'd have someone meet them up at White Dog Cave. Eventually.

"Idiotic bureaucracy," he said. "She said to be sure and let them know right away if we found we really needed help. Now, how in the heck could we do that? Send smoke signals?"

Perry tensed. If only he still had the cellular

phone that used to be part of his life back in St. Louis! What if Lauren had really been seriously hurt? His jaw set, and his foot pressed down even harder on the accelerator.

"Easy, son," Pops said gently. "She'll be all right. It *could* be that she just had trouble with the van, you know. We'll get her home safely."

But tension underlay Pops's consoling words. Perry thought of Glory's "feelings" and wondered if that sort of thing could be as contagious as it seemed to be right at this point.

"I'm falling in love with her, Pops."

"I know that, son. And don't slow up on my account. I love her too."

The tears seemed to wash away some of the cold despair that had penetrated Lauren's aching bones and clouded her mind. She sniffled and took a deep breath, trying to think logically.

By now, surely, Glory would be wondering what had happened to her. And maybe by now someone would be looking for her. But would they think to look in the right place? Maybe. Maybe if they saw her van. Maybe if they saw Charlie.

So maybe every few minutes she should

shout, as long as her voice held out. Just in case.

She tried a tentative "hallooo" and then added a drawn-out "heeelp." Eerie, how the sound bounced off the rocks and came back to haunt her. It made her feel more alone than ever.

And if no one came — what? She'd starve to death. She might go mad and claw at the limestone around her, and fifty years from now someone would find her outstretched skeletal fingers scrabbling uselessly at her rocky prison. With a great mental effort she slammed the door on that particular horrible fantasy and shouted once again, praying the sound would reach someone.

But the dismal specters of her imagination were still rattling at the door.

Even if her bones were neatly interred in a conventional coffin in a conventional cemetery, who would come to mourn, anyway? Auntie Nell was gone. Lily Mae would bring flowers from her garden, and Pops would wipe his eyes, and Nels would shake his head in sorrow and go find someone else to pursue. Ernie Campbell would probably dance on her grave. Glory would cry. How would Perry react? That question brought another spate of tears and a feeling of ineffable loss and sadness.

Perry. If she ever got out of here, she'd throw herself at him shamelessly, love him right out of that stubborn shell of his, help him face whatever demons haunted his past. If she ever got out of here.

She didn't want to be alone anymore. Always, she'd stood pretty much on her own, except for the steadying presence of Auntie Nell, carving her way — alone. Self-sufficient, that's what she was. But she'd never been as alone as she was right now, and she knew she never wanted to be so alone again.

If she ever got out of this — this mess. She shouted again over a lump in her throat that felt like — like rock.

"Go straight down the road till you come to the broken-down split-rail fence," Jake said without preamble, scrambling into the rear seat of Perry's car. "Hope I'm wrong, but I've got an awful hunch. I know the place pretty good, though. Let's go."

They took off with a spinning of wheels that sent Jake tumbling sharply back in the seat. "Whoa, Perry, go easy! Watch out for the chickens! Can't see the turn if you're going too fast, and three minutes ain't gonna make no difference. You got ropes? Flashlights?"

Perry assured him that they had supplies,

introduced Pops, and tried very hard to slow down.

"There it is, just beyond the crooked oak. Don't tear the rear end out of this fancy car now — that's a miserable road." He paused, apparently sizing up Perry's mood pretty accurately. "Fine young woman, she is. Don't worry, Perry. We'll find her."

Perry heard the barking even before he reached the glade. Charlie? Could it be Charlie? It had to be Charlie. . . .

Then he saw the van, the picnic basket, the dog. He pulled up, sounding the horn in a series of short blasts. If she were at the edge of the woods or behind the van, she'd hear him and come running over, asking what on earth they were doing here.

But she didn't appear. Charlie charged the car, barking; then he ran toward the stony bluff at the far side of the glade. Jake cussed efficiently and colorfully, words that fit Perry's mood exactly. "Sign's down," he growled, kicking at fallen boards that lay near the rock fissure. *White Dog Caverns*, it said. *Dangerous. Keep out.*

"Hills are riddled with these darned caves." Jake shook his head. "Just like Swiss cheese. And some fool kid or tourist is forever getting lost." He looked at Charlie, who was standing at the entrance with a baleful look and an equally baleful combination of bark and howl.

"Looks like Lauren was one of the fools," Pops said quietly. "Easy, Charlie. We'll get her. Why 'White Dog Cavern,' anyway?"

"Was kinda hoping you wouldn't ask that. Some kid — about a hundred years ago, it was — got lost in there. Him and his dog, an old white mutt. Never found 'em, but for years people have seen a big, old white ghost dog wandering around the caves. . . . Oh, shucks, Perry, hand me that flashlight and quit looking like a man on the way to his own hanging. We'll find her. At least," he added almost inaudibly, "I sure hope we will."

Chapter Ten

Charlie refused to enter the cave with them. "Useless critter," Jake muttered. Pops stayed outside the entrance to the caverns with the dog — "Just in case she shows up out here after all," Jake told him, while Perry and Jake took rope, flashlight, first-aid kit, and a wary hopefulness into the first of the passageways.

There were eerie echoes in response to their shouts. The rough, damp stones held no footprints, only silence and shadows. Perry shivered with more than cold or damp. Lauren could be injured, could be unconscious, could be . . . dead.

And he'd never told her he loved her.

He called her name desperately once more.

"Don't get a case of the cave-crazies now, boy," Jake told him. "Come on. Turn left up here where it narrows out. Cockamamy thing to do, comin' in here alone. Fool outlander trick. . . ."

Cave-crazies. Perry swallowed hard, following Jake, having a sudden horrifying realization of what it would be like to be literally buried alive deep within the earth. Their flashlights threw grotesque shadows that flickered and jumped before them.

Cave-crazies. A red-hot surge of determination and strength rocketed through him, and he shouted her name again. But this time his voice wasn't hoarse. It was a roar, and echoes bounced back at him like taunting, furious ghosts — and something more.

"Quit trying to break my eardrums and just listen," Jake growled. "I think we got it right this time."

Almost unbelieving, Perry listened, holding his breath. And, yes — that was Lauren's voice. "We're coming!" he bellowed and recklessly half slid, half leaped toward the sweet sound of that voice, ignoring Jake's advice to slow down.

When his flashlight picked her out, huddled against the rocks, with her white face turned toward him, he'd never seen a vision quite so terrible and yet so beautiful. She was streaked with mud from head to toe; her arm was scraped and bloody; there were traces of blood and of tears smearing the mud across her cheeks. When she tried to stand, turning toward them with swollen eyelids almost closed against the brightness of their lights, her leg seemed to give out beneath her, and she almost fell.

"What took you so long?" she whispered before he caught her in his arms and held her close, kissing mud, blood, and tears and murmuring a whole torrent of words that even he couldn't quite understand — but that, for some reason, she could.

She clung to him, half laughing, half crying. Somebody said something about being a darn fool, but he wasn't sure whether it was him or Jake or Lauren herself, or maybe all three. . . . There were anxious words about her injuries, thankful words, and practical words about getting her out of there. Afterward he was never able to remember who said exactly what, but someone had whispered *my love, my love,* and he was sure it wasn't Jake.

Walking was impossible for her, so he picked her up and carried her. She nestled her head against his neck and cried a little, gently, silently, and they weren't tears of pain.

Lauren's own memories of her emergence from darkness to blinding light were a happy jumble of relief, love, and gratitude. Perry knelt beside her, out in the blindingly beautiful sunshine, brushing soothing fingers across her face. She had a feeling that verged on delirious happiness, especially when she heard him say something about her being his "poor, muddy, beautiful love."

And Pops was there, busy trying to keep Charlie from leaping on her in his own joy.

"Now, child," he kept saying. "Now, Charlie —" She thought she saw a mist in Pops's eyes, and she smiled at him through the stiff mask that was her face.

"I'll be all right," she said to all of them.

"We'll get you to the clinic, to be sure," Perry said.

"No clinic. I'll be all right," she repeated stubbornly. "I'm just sorry to have caused you all this trouble."

She must have said she was sorry a dozen times on the drive back to Piney Ridge. Pops, driving Lauren's van, took Jake back to his cabin. Perry bundled Lauren into his own car as if she were a piece of very breakable fine china, allowing Charlie to leap into the backseat.

She murmured something about Charlie messing up the car, but Perry pointed out, logically, that she'd mess it up worse, and she couldn't argue with that. Charlie laid his black muzzle on the back of the front seat and watched first one of them and then the other.

"You gave us such a scare." Perry's voice sounded more caring than angry. "Such a terrible scare."

"I'm sorry," she said again. And then, from a feeling of dreamy unreality, added, "I thought I'd die in there. I really did think

I would. And I saw a dog, but it wasn't Charlie."

"Not a white dog?" Perry asked, looking a little startled.

"I think so, but it was probably just my eyes playing tricks on me." Perry looked strangely thoughtful as she continued, "I want to go home and change clothes and put my feet up. No clinic, Perry. We have elastic bandages, and I need a bath more than I need a doctor."

He looked as if he wanted to argue, but he gave in. "I'll wash your back," he offered with a hint of mischief in his eyes.

That didn't sound like Perry. She grinned. Though maybe, she told herself, she shouldn't be surprised, after that emotional rescue. The warm, outgoing side of his nature had conquered the cool reserve — for now. She wondered how long it would last.

And she had to stop herself from saying, "Please do." It was an almost irresistible offer. "Thank you, but I believe I can manage," she said, trying to sound prim and spoiling the effect with an unrestrainable throaty chuckle.

There was only one customer in the shop when they arrived, and Glory, fluttering about like a distressed sparrow, managed to conclude the sale of a slipware pie pan with polite but hasty dispatch. Flipping the Open sign to Closed, she locked the door and flew up the back stairs in pursuit of Perry and a hobbling Lauren, nonstop questions bubbling from her.

It was Glory, listening wide-eyed to the explanations, who drew the bathwater, got Lauren's favorite shampoo from the closet in the hall, clucked soothingly, and directed Perry to call Lily Mae *right away*. Obediently, obviously feeling shooed off so that Glory could get on with taking care of Lauren, he departed.

"But I'll be back soon," he promised. "With a wider bandage for your ankle. Don't go away." He looked back over his shoulder at her as he left the room, and the look that he gave her made her feel every bit as good as all of Glory's ministrations.

In a blur of relief, Lauren let the dirt and darkness of the caves swirl away down the drain with the gurgling bathwater, allowed Glory to brush her wet hair into submission and put antiseptic on her scraped arms, slathered herself with skin softeners, slipped into her white caftan, and felt almost at peace.

Hazily she heard her van pull back into its place beside her back door, and then she heard Pops's heavy tread on the stairs.

"Glory's fixing you soup and a salad, child," he said softly. "Perry just pulled in too, and he's going to run me home. So you just rest, hear?" He kissed her on top of the head, his moustache tickling at her forehead. She smiled mistily at him, and he patted her shoulder, a benevolent grandfather, and was gone.

By the time she'd finished the soup and salad, Perry was back, talking to Glory down in the kitchen. She would go down and join them. . . . But the idea was a futile one. She managed to hobble, biting her lip against the pain, only as far as the door to her room before Perry had bounded up the stairs, taken her firmly by the arms, and guided her back to her rocking chair.

"Stay out!" he growled at her. It was a nice, soft growl, though — more like a purr, she thought, and beamed at him. "Glory's going to be off now, and I'm going to baby-sit."

Lauren was about to protest the use of the word "baby-sit" when Glory's bright face appeared around Perry's left arm. "You do what he says, now, hear?" Glory said. "I surely am glad you're safe now, and I'll see you tomorrow." She gave them both an amused, approving — and somehow very knowing — look and was gone.

"Bright kid," Perry said. "Perceptive. And you're looking much better." He bent over and kissed the top of her head, much as Pops had done. She tried tilting her head back, so that the kiss might slip downward to a more interesting position, but he pulled back. With a smile, but he pulled back.

He pulled over a footstool and sat down, lifting her sore foot with a firm, light touch and putting it on his knees. "Let's get that ankle retaped," he said. "Very pretty ankle," he added. "And only a little swelling. Have you iced it at all?"

"Glory insisted on that. Until I had to tell her I was getting frostbite." She pulled the hem of the caftan up a few inches so she could watch the tips of his fingers run lightly around the painful area. "Touch it in the wrong place, and I'll break this lamp over your head," she warned him. But at that moment it wasn't painful at all. Odd, she'd never known that an ankle could give off delicious sensations.

He chuckled. "It seems to have thawed out now," he observed, cupping ankle and calf between two large, warm hands.

"It certainly has," she agreed. Sitting back, closing her eyes, she savored the unexpected bliss of having an ankle taped.

"There," he said after a moment, looking up into eyes that were dreamily warm. "That should do it for now."

"For now. Thank you." The expression in her eyes had moved somehow to her mouth — those sweet, full, eminently kissable lips that curved up now in a warm smile. He longed to taste them, to see if they were as warm and sweet as they looked. He closed his own eyes momentarily. He wanted to hold her and caress her and tell her how much she meant to him. He wanted to talk to her, to bring those old dark shadows out into the light and hope that she'd help him rid himself of them.

"And then," he said, as if he'd been speaking his thoughts aloud, "there's the matter of that break-in. But this isn't the right time for all that. You need rest, and I should go."

She looked disappointed. He wondered how she'd look if she'd heard the first part of his thoughts as well as the last. "Thank you, Perry," was all she said.

"I'll be back tomorrow, he promised. He stood up, and before he could stop himself, he bent over the rocking chair and kissed her, cupping her chin in his hand and finding the warmth and the sweetness even more poignant than he'd thought they'd be.

He stood straight and shook himself slightly, trying to rein in his galloping thoughts and feelings. "There are a great many things we'll have to discuss at a more propitious time," he said.

Even to his own ears, his voice was husky and sounded not at all like the cool and neutral attorney, as he'd intended. He thought he heard a small, sleepy laugh behind him as he left the room, back straight. But he didn't dare turn around to make sure.

Lauren awoke the next morning with a peculiar unreal mist blurring her consciousness. A combination of dreams, perhaps, a confusion of waking thoughts?

Closing her eyes, opening them again, she stared at the faint shadows on her ceiling, thoughts beginning to clear. Being lost in the cave had not been part of a dream. Yesterday flooded back into her consciousness.

All of yesterday. Including Perry and his touch, and his kiss, and his ridiculous parting statement. Well, it wasn't the statement so much — that had been vintage Perry Lucas — it had been the tone of voice. She'd rattled him, all right. Of course, she hadn't been exactly unrattled herself.

Charlie was woofing in the kitchen; Glory must have left him in there. She'd have to go down and let him out. Oops. There wasn't, she discovered as she sat up, an inch of her that didn't ache. It was quite a while before she could even get dressed, let alone think about navigating her stairs. Thank heavens for her caftans — she didn't have to try to shove her ridiculous fat foot into jeans. She hopped;

she hobbled; she wobbled. By the time she'd reached the kitchen and Charlie's enthusiastic good morning, she was sure she must look like an arthritic elderly kangaroo.

Lauren shared her toast with Charlie, one eye on the clock. What time did Perry get up? She wanted him here, wanted to talk to him. And was this, she wondered with a grin, a propitious time? But when the phone rang shortly after seven-thirty, it was Glory, telling her not to walk, to wait for her, to play invalid today. Lauren started to argue and then decided playing invalid might have its merits. Besides, Glory's voice sounded worried, strained. Lauren felt a pang of guilt for having caused so much anxiety the day before.

Lily Mae called a few minutes later. Then Pops, then Nels, who wanted to talk about this adventure she'd had, which he'd heard about through the grapevine. She cut him off after assuring him she was just fine. Perry had probably been trying to call her all this time, for heaven's sake. She'd call him — right now.

His answering machine clicked in after the fourth ring. "Darn it, I don't *want* to talk to your machine," she told it plaintively. "It has no heart and soul. Call me as soon as you can." Then she added in a small voice, "This is Lauren." But of course he'd know that. Of course. But where was he?

A small but exceedingly sharp needle of un-certainty stabbed at the back of her mind. What *were* all those things he'd said they needed to talk about? Why did she feel like a schoolgirl in the throes of a first crush? *Play it cool, Lauren,* she told herself. *Get busy with something else. Don't think about it right now.*

When Glory arrived a short time later, Lauren was ensconced on her favorite, some-what ratty old wicker chaise on the back porch. Papers and books cluttered the table beside her and spilled onto the floor, and none of her concentration had taken her mind from wondering where Perry was.

"Now, that's just plain dumb," Glory said crossly. Lauren looked up at her, surprised. Glory was never cross. "Carting all that stuff out here by yourself. You should have waited for me."

"I sort of took my time at it," Lauren an-swered vaguely, studying Glory's face. The girl's eyes looked puffy, and no magic dust swirled around her today. "Is something wrong, Glory?"

"You should have waited for me." Glory's tone was stubborn. "That's all." She thrust her hands into the pockets of her slim jeans and looked down at her feet. "That's all," she repeated. Her shoulders drooped dejectedly under the bright summer shirt. When she glanced back up at Lauren and tried to smile the corners of her mouth didn't lift far enough to dimple her cheeks.

"All right," Lauren said gently, suddenly feeling like an older sister. "Some days just aren't as good as others, are they? Go get yourself a glass of orange juice or a cup of coffee and come back out here and sit down with me for a while."

Lauren watched Glory obediently trudge away and thought, *Little sister. I'm not alone after all, am I? She's like family.*

"I'll let you answer the phone if it rings, Glory," she told the girl when she appeared once more with her juice. "I'm sort of expecting a call from Perry Lucas, and you can catch the phone more easily than I can."

"Men!" Glory's unexpected vehemence as she plopped into the porch rocker beside Lauren, almost spilling her orange juice, startled Lauren. "Men! You just can't trust any of them!"

So that was it. Funny, she hadn't thought of it before, but of course Glory must have a boyfriend, unless the boys at Piney Ridge High School were all blind boneheaded fools.

Lauren tried patience and gentle cajoling, and eventually the story came out. Kenny was a beautiful big hunk of a guy, Glory said. He was off at his first year at State College, studying to be a veterinarian. He was two years older than Glory.

"And then he comes home this summer," Glory said, "and says there's this girl —" Her voice faltered.

It was no good telling her how many other fish there were in the sea. Besides, Piney Ridge was just a small pond, not the sea. Lauren made sympathetic noises deep in her throat. After all, she was beginning to know how it felt to care about a difficult man.

Huge tears brimmed at the corner of Glory's eyes. They swelled, puddled, and spilled over at last down her cheeks. "But that's not all, anyway. I was going to go to State after I graduate. And maybe Kenny and I could have worked it all out. But not now."

"You're not going? You wanted to study accounting —"

"Oh, I did and I do. It's just that — well, I have an older brother who's in college now."

Lauren frowned. "You mean, your parents can't help out as much as you'd hoped."

"Dad was laid off for a while last year. I thought I could work part-time, and I think I could get a grant or a scholarship, but still. . . ." Sitting up straight and squaring her shoulders, Glory tried to force a smile. It didn't work well. "Anyway, that's not your problem — you have enough of your own, and I should be helping to get these things in order. Anything you want me to do besides coding in some of the newer things?"

"Not that I can think of," Lauren told her. "Glory, you know — maybe things will work out. One way or another."

"Oh, yes, they surely will," she answered with a crooked smile. "They surely will, one way or another."

At five Glory closed the door and flipped the sign to Closed. Lauren had watched her all day, sympathizing, not wanting to say too much, worrying about the girl. She watched her leave with regret for the lost Tinkerbelle sparkle.

Easing her way awkwardly into the kitchen, she popped a frozen dinner into her microwave with reluctance. She wasn't hungry, but she knew she should have something. . . .

Perry hadn't called. She wondered, staring idly out the window and chewing on what seemed to be cardboard meat loaf, whether her lack of appetite was a reaction to that fact. The oddly hollow feeling inside her wasn't a hunger for food.

Twice she reached for the phone; twice she pulled her hand back.

She gave up on the cardboard. She had to *do* something — something besides sit here wondering why he didn't call. The slanted shadows on the green-gold field behind her house spoke of passing time as well as of a beautiful soft evening. Her ankle didn't feel all that bad now, did it? Maybe it was foolish, but —

"Come on, Charlie. Let's go for a little walk." He was the one creature she knew who wouldn't tell her she shouldn't do that.

The tree-studded slope was smooth and the cane she'd rescued from her stock helped. Charlie looked disappointed that she didn't race with him, but eventually wandered off on his own small journeys of important investigation.

The weakened muscles of her ankle sabotaged her with a sudden stab of pain, and she sat down on the warm, fragrant grass to rest and think. One part of her mind registered the peaceful dusky loveliness around her, while another part moped in a corner like a sulky child who hadn't been given a promised treat.

"That's ridiculous," she muttered aloud. "Just ridiculous. He'll call me. I'll call him. We'll call each other."

A sharp bark from Charlie jarred her from this unprofitable circular track, and she looked up to see what he had found.

He stood motionless, staring at a clump of

trees at the side of the clearing where shadows had gathered more and more deeply as the sun dimmed. He didn't seem upset, but his tail wasn't wagging, either, and Lauren frowned, peering into the shadows.

Shivers light as moths' wings spread across her neck and shoulders. First the break-in. Then that living death in the cave. . . . Now was someone lurking, watching? She called the dog. He obeyed reluctantly, still watching the trees, a growl seemingly stuck deep in his throat. At least she had his protection.

"Is someone there?" she asked when Charlie had reached her and she could stroke his back to reassure them both. "Who is it?" Her voice almost, but not quite, wavered.

A slight, exceedingly nonthreatening figure materialized slowly among the shadows. "I hope I didn't frighten you, Miss Byrd?" the figure said hesitantly, coming toward her, and Lauren breathed a sigh of relief and let her tense muscles relax.

"Mrs. Campbell. I couldn't see who you were."

"Oh, I didn't want to startle that dog. I didn't know if he might attack or something?"

"No. He's a pussycat, actually. Sit, Charlie."

"You're sure?" Lou Campbell advanced

slowly, watching Charlie. "Oh, and" — she looked a bit frightened of her own words — "I do wish you'd call me Lou? Not Mrs. Campbell."

Lauren wondered, rather cynically, whether the poor woman didn't like being Mrs. Campbell. It was an unkind thought, and she squelched it. "And you must call me Lauren," she said softly. "Were you looking for me, then, Lou?"

"Sort of. I mean, I've heard — you know how things get around? — that you've had some awful things happening, and I just wanted to be neighborly and see if you were all right?"

News networks in small towns, Lauren reflected wryly, were quicker than satellite coverage. "I'm fine, except for a sore ankle, and thank you." Did Ernie know Lou had a neighborly streak? She seriously doubted it.

"I wanted to say, too," Lou said, turning her head shyly away from Lauren, "that you mustn't take too much offense at Ernie. He's like a little banty rooster, gets his feathers all ruffled and makes a lot of noise, but he calms down." She looked back at Lauren, eyes inquisitive, nose twitching a little. "Maybe he's sort of like your dog — his bark's worse than his bite?"

"Maybe," Lauren murmured. "Maybe we

can work things out."

"Oh, you will, you will. It'll all work out, you'll see? And I've wanted to come over and welcome you for quite a while now, but there just hasn't been a good time. I did sneak over a couple of times, though." Lauren could have sworn that the older woman almost giggled. "Did you know?"

"No," Lauren said blankly. And then it dawned on her. "Gingersnaps?" she said. "Gingersnaps and brownies?" For heaven's sake, now she was sounding just like Lou, mixing sentences with question marks.

A beatific smile lit Lou's face. "You liked them, then?" she asked eagerly.

"How could I help it? Won't you sit down and talk for a few minutes, Lou? So that I can thank you properly?"

"Oh, now see? It's just like I told Ernie and told him, you're a well-brought-up nice young woman, aren't you?"

"Did you really say that?" Lauren asked, pleased, and the two of them sat on the grass, full of questions, while the light faded gradually and Charlie snoozed contentedly beside them.

"So you found nothing." The voice was thoughtful. "You know, I wonder if that's bad or good, but we have to be sure."

"I don't know where else we can look. Anyway, the dingbat keeps papers in all kinds of places. No order to it at all. The stuff that hasn't been sorted looks like a Pentagon out-basket."

"You're making excuses. Still . . . there's the outside chance that Jacoby destroyed anything incriminating before he died. Or that the Piney Ridge dealer stumbled across the stuff, didn't know what it was, and tossed it. It was coded — probably wouldn't have meant anything to her."

"Want us to back off, then?"

"Don't be so eager. I didn't say that — yet. Maybe you gave up too soon, or maybe you haven't got enough sense to know what kind of evidence you're looking for."

"Hey, I'm tired of your put-downs. If you think you can do a better job, *you* do it. Just make sure I get what you owe me."

"Oh, I will, I will. But I think it would be a good idea to get someone else to sort through all that stuff that was sold at auction — someone a little closer to the whole thing, someone who has something to lose if certain details come to light. Someone I'm going to have to put a bit more pressure on. Stay in touch."

A snort. "Good luck. You'll need it."

"Yes. And, er, the same to you."

Chapter Eleven

A silvery crescent moon was just beginning to lift above the tallest trees when Lauren limped up her back steps. She was smiling inside, and her heart felt warm. Lou Campbell was shy and sensitive but not weak.

Ernie was just a — a certain type of man, Lou had told Lauren hesitantly. Living with him wasn't always easy, but he had his good side. Lauren wondered where that side could possibly be, but she didn't want to ask the question out loud.

Give him time, Lou had said. He'd come around.

Maybe that was good advice. It was, after all, basically what Perry had told her too. And Lou had said, very bravely, Lauren thought, that she certainly wasn't going to hide her friendship with Lauren. He'd have to accept it, wouldn't he? And pretty soon he'd accept Lauren too, and they'd all just forget about that old property-line problem?

As Perry had predicted.

Lauren took a can of Coke from the refrigerator and collapsed into the old rocking chair in the corner, Charlie at her feet. Just where was Perry, anyway? She glared at the silent phone, hanging there on the wall, and it responded, after about ten seconds of her malevolent stare, by starting to ring.

Heartened at her ability to work miracles, Lauren hobbled awkwardly to answer. Her "Hello, this is Country Blues," contained a hint of pain and hope — and a slight echo of Lou Campbell's voice.

"Lauren? For heaven's sake, where have you been? I've been trying for the last hour to get through. Are you all right?"

"Yes, thank you, Perry," she answered sweetly. He must be truly worried about her to sound so aggravated. "I'm just fine. I was just outside in back for a while —"

"Walking around on that ankle? Do I have to come over there and stand over you to make sure you take care of yourself?"

"Yes, thank you, Perry," she repeated in the same voice. And then added, aggrieved, "Darn it, where have *you* been all day?"

"Truce," he answered with a weary laugh. "I'm sorry I wasn't here. Had to arrange a power of attorney for a client in Beaverton and then ran to the county archives twice before I was done. Tried to call you this morning, but the phone was busy."

Yes, it had been. "You're forgiven." It was probably a good thing he couldn't see her starry-eyed smile. Good heavens, she'd have to get her emotions a little more under control. This wasn't like the coolly detached Lauren Byrd she'd always known. "If you're not too tired, please do come over," she told him. The words were reasonably cool and detached, but the tone wasn't.

"You're sure?" His voice echoed the warmth in her own.

"Positive."

"Give me about twenty minutes."

She hung up and grinned idiotically at the dozing dog. With the help of the cane, hardly feeling the protestation of the muscles in her ankle and calf, she pulled herself up the stairs: Freshen up, slip into — let's see — the jungly green caftan, put on jade earrings, brush her hair, add a touch of perfume. . . .

That darned elastic bandage. Good sense won out over vanity, and she didn't try to remove it. She inched cautiously back down to her kitchen, arriving just in time to hear Charlie rouse himself enough to woof a friendly welcome toward the back door.

"Come on in," she called softly, bracing herself against the table. Her knees felt a bit weak, and her heart was pounding harder than usual — no doubt the exertion of going up and down stairs with that injured ankle, she told herself, but knew better.

Perry slipped in through the screen door and stopped, taking her in from head to toe with a slight smile and almost fathomless eyes. "You look beautiful," he said. The smile faded, and a mock sternness took over the dark eyes. "You shouldn't leave that door unlatched," he told her. "Anyone could walk right in."

"Like you just did. But only because Charlie knows you," she told him. And added, "Thank you." She wasn't absolutely sure what she was thanking him for, but it really didn't matter. Especially when he walked over to her and took her in his arms, holding her gently and protectively, burying his face in her hair and murmuring something that she couldn't quite make out.

His lips moved from her hair lightly across her cheek, and she turned her head and tilted her chin up to catch his lips against her own. The weakness in her knees and the racing of her heart intensified tenfold. Vaguely she became aware that her eyes were filling with tears.

Perry's lips brushed momentarily across her cheek, and he drew his head back, startled. He looked down at her in concern and saw the two tears tracing a path over her cheeks. For heaven's sake, what had he done to her? With a sense of alarm, he drew back.

"Tears?" he managed to say. "Did I hurt you?" She was shaking her head, but a small sense of reality was beginning to return. Her injured ankle — "My poor darling," he said. "You shouldn't be standing here like this, with that ankle of yours —"

Her eyes opened wider, tears caught in the thick lashes. But there was a hint of laughter in those eyes, and the corners of her mouth, lips rosy and now very full, turned up just a fraction.

"What ankle?" she asked dreamily and then sighed and brushed at the dampness on her cheeks. "Those are tears of joy." There was wonder in her voice. "That's never happened to me before."

He wanted to ask a number of questions about that statement, but perhaps not right at this moment. Right now he should make her sit down, let common sense take over, take a look at that ankle, try to have a rational conversation with her, if possible. Was he capable of truly rational conversation? He doubted it.

Somehow the process of getting her off her feet ended up quite pleasantly with both of them sitting in the big rocking chair, Lauren's head snuggled against his neck. So much for rational conversation.

"It just makes you wonder, though," he said

after a few moments of just sitting blissfully, cradling her softness.

"Wonder what?"

"Why people fall in love."

"People in general, or particular people?"

"Well, particular people, I guess," he said and kissed her eyebrow. Her eyebrow was safer than those lips. He was beginning not to trust himself at all, and there were things that he felt he should say. "I do love you, you know." That was one of the things, of course. But there was so much more. . . .

"And I love you." Distractingly, she kissed his earlobe. "Since you brought it up, why should you fall in love with me?"

"Because you're beautiful," he answered promptly. She made a disparaging little noise. "You're warm and intelligent and — and —" He groped for words, then chuckled. "And because you're an antiques dealer who can find steamboat memorabilia for me, of course. I saw it yesterday after we brought you home. The steamboat model with the not-for-sale tag. Was it supposed to be a surprise for me, or were you going to keep it for yourself?"

Lauren sat very still and silent for a few seconds and then murmured something about "joint custody" that he didn't quite catch. He liked the sound of it, though.

"Turnabout's fair play," he told her. "I

don't really see why you should have decided to love a difficult lug like me."

"You *are* difficult at times," she said, drawing away and considering him thoughtfully. "Challenging. Hard to understand. Changeable. But there's something underneath all that —"

"I certainly hope so." Was this the time to tell her about his uncertainties about himself, his fear of stress, the reasons for his changeability? "Lauren —"

"You're different," she said musingly. "I thought I was in love — oh, two or three times, maybe. But it wasn't like this."

He kissed her other eyebrow.

"You know," she said slowly, tracing his jawline with a feather-light finger, "I never had a traditional family when I was growing up. It was mostly just Auntie Nell and me. Sometimes I thought I was missing out, and sometimes it seemed best just the way it was. Maybe that's why I never really fell in love."

"I have lots and lots of family I can share with you."

She nodded absently, but she still seemed to be putting the pieces of her memories together. "And then there were the Lees." She stopped, frowning.

"Mmm?" he encouraged. A shadow seemed to pass over her face. "Who were the Lees?"

"They lived around the corner from us. When I was very small, we spent a few holidays with them, and I thought it was nice to be with a family. Then it all changed, and I was . . . frightened."

This was obviously important to her. "Frightened," he repeated, shifting his weight so that he could look into her eyes.

But she stared at the vintage vinyl that covered her kitchen floor. "Mr. Lee lost his job and couldn't find another. Mrs. Lee had a job, but it wasn't enough. He started to drink. . . . Well, eventually he started to take out his frustrations on her. And on the two children. And one night he killed a liquor-store owner. Liquor and stress, they said."

"Liquor and stress," Perry repeated hollowly.

"It stuck with me, the horror of it. I was only eleven. I think I made up my mind then to make it on my own. . . ."

No, this wasn't the time to tell her about his own past. He heard a deep sigh and realized it had come from him. "Lauren," he managed, "there's a lot you don't know about me. But you can be sure I'd never hurt you."

"Well, of course you wouldn't!" she said. She was back with him now, looking questions at him — questions that he wasn't ready to answer. "Perry, what is it?"

"Nothing, my love. Nothing that can't wait. I think we're both tired tonight. It would be best if I left now."

"You're sure of that?" He could hear the injured pride — and the curiosity. Conflicting emotions tore at him.

They were standing now, and he took her, carefully, into his arms once again. "I love you," he said. His voice was uneven, and he gave himself a mental shake. "There are things we have to talk about and then plans to make," he added, trying to sound common-sensical and levelheaded. "And I want to help you go through the things that Dutch and Harry brought by. We haven't even talked about the break-in, and I have this absurd desire to try to take care of you. You, of all people, who apparently can usually take very good care of yourself."

"Except for stumbling into deep, dark, im-penetrable caves and into love with deep, dark, impenetrable men," she said. There was an edge to her voice, but her eyes were soft. "All right. We'll talk about it all later. I'd appreciate your help — maybe you can make some sense of the whole thing. I certainly can't."

"I'll call you tomorrow and come over Friday, if that's all right. Could we go out for dinner before we start sleuthing?"

She smiled and nodded, and he had to kiss her again, several times, before he could make himself walk out into the darkness.

Lauren watched him go, puzzled and uncertain. Could they work it out, whatever the problem might be? There was definitely a problem there, something he didn't want to talk about.

Well, with a few psychological and physical wiles she'd take care of that, by golly. She hoped.

Although it was late, she sat for a long time in the kitchen rocking chair. Life in the hills wasn't as uncomplicated as she'd hoped. And she should have known better. Auntie Nell had told her and told her: "Life can be complicated, so you'd better be ready to deal with it." Up until now she'd been able to do that.

Now she wanted somebody to stand beside her to face the complications. And that fact was a complication in itself.

Nels showed up the next morning, not like himself at all — full of concern and advice, his usual brashness subdued.

"I'm fine, honestly," she assured him. "I'm being careful. No real harm done — thanks to Perry and Jake and Pops."

He watched her closely as she poured coffee into thick mugs. She wondered if her face had reflected the warmth that came from within her on that last sentence, for Nels frowned and looked chagrined — jealous, maybe. Inwardly she sighed.

He carried the mugs to the table for her, avoiding her eyes, the slight frown hovering like a gray cloud. "Perry Lucas. The knight in shining armor. Just be sure it isn't tarnished."

Sudden anger gripped her. "And just what does that mean?" she snapped. Nels and his sly digs — it might be just a touch of nasty male jealousy, but she couldn't let him get away with it.

"Nothing. Sorry." He didn't look sorry. He shrugged, half smiled at her. "Just old rumors that don't mean anything."

"Then don't bring it up." She should let it drop, but she felt both defensive and curious. Angry at both herself and Nels, she glared at him.

"I suppose I shouldn't," he said reluctantly. "But where there's smoke . . . you know. They say Perry had some pretty deep emotional troubles in St. Louis and worked too hard —"

"Perry had a difficult time when his wife died," she said through clenched teeth. "But he's levelheaded and honest, and you should be ashamed of yourself for spreading gossip and rumors." Getting to her feet, she gripped her cane ferociously.

Nels rose too, backing toward the door and looking apprehensive. "Sorry. Should keep my mouth shut. See you later, all right?" But he didn't look sorry. There was a hint of smugness around his mouth when he slipped out the door and down the steps. She watched him go, speechless with anger and something else — an unidentifiable niggling that was the first cousin to worry.

Nels was jealous. That was all. But there *did* seem to be something Perry wouldn't talk about. There was still an invisible webby curtain between them that she couldn't quite penetrate.

Nothing to worry about, she told herself firmly. She sat down at the kitchen table with her chin propped in her hands, ready to fret and stew, anyway. Charlie, sensing her mood and knowing that the panacea for all worries was a frolic with his tennis ball, grabbed it and came to sit beside her with an inviting gleam in his eye. She scratched him absently behind the ears. Neither physically nor psychologically was she in any shape for a frolic.

Not with a dog and a tennis ball, anyway.

An unearthly noise sent her gloomy thoughts fleeing — a clatter that rattled, coughed, and gasped to a stop just outside.

There was no mistaking the sound of Lily Mae's old jalopy.

Lauren hadn't even hobbled as far as the screen door before Lily Mae materialized beyond it, her arms full of something frothy and pastel. "Baby quilt," Lily Mae explained as she let herself in. "Go sit down, child. I can manage for myself. Finished this last night and had to come into town, anyway, so I brought it by. Sit."

The word was pronounced with such authority that both Charlie and Lauren obeyed. Lily Mae beamed.

"You don't look so poorly, after all. We'll find a good spot for this. Like it, do you?" Lauren was running gentle fingers over the delicate softness, cooing a little. "Thought you would. Want me to stay around for a bit? About time to open, isn't it?"

Lauren managed to get a word in edgewise. "Thanks, Lily Mae. It's beautiful — put it on the quilt rack by the window. And I'll fix tea, if you can stay, but I can handle the shop all right."

"Well, if you think so." Lily Mae's voice floated back over her shoulder as she disappeared toward the living-room portion of the shop. "Yes, I'd like some tea, but you sit still while I fix it. I do know how, you know." She was back in the kitchen, eyes twinkling, almost immediately. "Thought I saw Nels's car rounding the corner just as I came up. Been to check on you, has he?"

Lauren opened her mouth, couldn't think of anything very nice to say, and closed it again rather abruptly.

"Mmm." Lily Mae turned the fire up under the teakettle and studied Lauren's face. "Looks like he got your goat. Probably telling you to stay out of caves and be more careful?"

"Not quite," Lauren managed. "Actually — it sounds silly, I suppose — but I think he's jealous."

"Of Perry," Lily Mae said immediately, nodding and looking ridiculously pleased. She brought the cups to the table and sat across from Lauren, smiling a small smile. "Well, stands to reason. He's wishing he'd been the one to haul you out of that cave instead of Perry, I reckon."

"Sometimes he — he annoys me."

"Nels, you mean. Yes, I can see that. And you've taken quite a shine to Perry, haven't you?" Lauren nodded reluctantly. "Well, now," the older woman said after a few minutes' thought, "I don't think Nels means any harm. He could be a pestiferous little rapscallion when he was a boy, but he kind of grew out of all that, like boys will. Works hard, has done well at Hawke's Nest."

Lauren's only reply was a deep sigh. She'd already asked Lily Mae about Perry's past, when Nels had first made his insidious sly hints, and Lily Mae knew nothing about it. It was just jealous shadows in Nels's mind, that's all. She straightened her shoulders, lifted her chin, and gave Lily Mae a weak smile. "I should just ignore Nels," she said.

"Pretty hard to do, I'd guess, if he hasn't quite outgrown his pestiferousness." Lily Mae stared down into her cup, as if tea leaves were scattered across the bottom, making predictions.

"Lots of females hereabouts that'd like to snare Nels. He's a well-favored man, in looks and money," Lily Mae said softly. "And in smarts too. Hawke's Nest was pretty run-down when Nels's daddy died and he took over. His older brother took off for Kansas City to work for some finance company — don't think he was much help. So — well, credit where credit's due, I always say."

She looked up at Lauren, smiling widely. "But somebody else is a-tuggin' on your heartstrings, right? And that's fine too, bless you, child." The "bless you" sounded like a genuine benediction and brought a prickle of tears to Lauren's eyes.

When Lily Mae left, Lauren limped to the

front porch and watched the old car rattle away down the tree-lined street, feeling strangely at peace — blessed, indeed.

The dark loneliness she'd felt in the depths of the caverns had been lightened by the glow of the friendships she felt around her — Pops, Lily Mae, Glory, and even Lou Campbell, of all people. They outbalanced Nels. And the warmest glow of all was definitely the one that Perry had wrapped around her. Feeling absurdly sentimental — and somehow protective toward Perry, silly as that might be — she flipped her door sign to Open. Sooner or later he'd share his secrets with her, and she'd understand.

Wouldn't he — wouldn't she?

"You know what I'd really like to do this evening?" Perry asked when he called a little after seven.

"Mmm . . . what?" Lauren asked, somewhat dreamily, closing her eyes and allowing her imagination to linger over possibilities.

"Go over all the boxes that Dutch and Harry brought — the things that you haven't catalogued, see if together we can find anything that might explain why someone would want to break in."

It wasn't exactly what Lauren hoped he'd say, but at least the word "together" was in

there. So she agreed, then managed the stairs
rather nicely so she could slip into her silvery
caftan and brush her hair until it glowed silky
and alive with light. By the time his car pulled
into the driveway, she'd put out crackers and
cheese and the expensive bottle of wine she'd
stashed for a rainy day. No matter that there
wasn't a cloud in the sky. . . .

Perry brought up a couple of boxes from
the cellar, lugged in the big box from the
butler's pantry, insisted on going through
what remained in the trunk — which wasn't
much, since she and Glory had catalogued
most of it and put it out for sale.

"It doesn't make sense," she said after an
hour or so of futile scrabbling through everything from buttons to a collection of postcards. "Maybe it was all imagination?" She
twirled her wineglass between her thumb and
forefinger. He'd had scarcely two glasses of
wine, and outside of a quick — much too quick
— embrace when he'd come in, his manner
was curiously detached.

"You're not the type to have silly flights
of imagination."

"Little do you know."

He looked up with a quick smile, as if he
had read her mind. "What about Charlie?"
he asked.

"That bothers me. Could someone he

216

doesn't even know talk him into the shed? Could anyone get close enough to put something in his food or water? He may be a kind of a lush puppy sometimes, but he *is* protective and — and it doesn't add up. Besides, Ernie said he heard him barking between nine and ten. Charlie was okay then, obviously. Hey, what about a tranquilizer gun?"

"You talked to Ernie?" he asked, ignoring her final question. It was almost an accusation.

"Not willingly. He called to complain, of course. I did talk to Lou, though." She told him about the encounter on the hillside. At least Perry looked pleased and approving about that.

"You'll see — the situation will resolve itself," he commented judiciously. The formal, old-fashioned Perry was back momentarily. Lauren stifled a giggle. Perry gave her a long look, thoughtful and assessing, and then his eyes softened in a way that made her heart lurch. "I worry about you. I don't like your being here alone, with something strange going on."

"I have Charlie. And Glory's here during the day."

He got up from the table and went to pour himself more coffee. She could almost see him hiding within himself once again, darn the man. *Out with it!* she wanted to shout. *Whatever it is that has short-circuited your emotiona thermostat, tell me!*

"Glory's working out well, then," he saic coolly, turning toward her.

Lauren tried to smile. She wouldn't push Not right now. But sooner or later. . . .

So she told him about Glory: her quick intelligence, her abilities — and her problems. "I just don't know whether to offer to help or not. I mean — Well, would the Mitchells be offended if I offered some financial assistance? Would I hurt their pride?"

"They'd be pleased, I think, and so would Glory. But is the shop doing that well?"

"I'm not that dependent on the shop. After all, a successful electronics firm doesn't sell for peanuts. I own this place outright and have good investments."

He made a strangled sound that brought her to her feet and to his side — almost without limping. Horrors, did he resent financially independent women? Some men did. "You're not upset?" she managed to ask before she was swept into his arms and held so closely she nearly yelped with surprise.

He was shaking. Well, one of them was, and she thought it was Perry. Then she realized that he was silently laughing, burying his head in her hair and nuzzling her ear.

218

"I hadn't realized that I'd fallen in love with — with a woman of substance." He'd finally said the magic word, after avoiding it all evening. He'd confirmed: He'd fallen in love.

And it was just a few minutes later that he asked her if she was really going to cry every time he kissed her. Because if she was, he said, the future certainly looked damp.

Chapter Twelve

Lauren awoke early the next morning, swimming up reluctantly through fragments o dreams that were almost too sweet to leave

But reality, her gradually waking mind anc heart told her, was pretty great too, and she might as well wake up. With a smile, remembering the night before, she opened her eyes

Perry had said he loved her, that his idea of paradise was to spend the rest of his life with her. All the right things, that's what he'c said.

Including admitting that he had a shadow in his past that he wanted to talk about. He'c fix dinner at his place Friday night and they'c talk, he said. That was wonderful, but she wanted to do more than talk. And, after all, what could he possibly say to pull her off the top of the rainbow she was dancing on?

But she must get out of bed and start attending to business, which today included Glory's future. Glory would be working with her just three hours today, and it might take that time and more to get the girl even to consider taking her offer of financial aid for college seriously. Lauren didn't even know

Glory's parents, but they might well be even more resistant than Glory. And she knew that Glory had a strong spark of pride that would probably make her say thank you, but you just can't do that.

"Oh, my goodness, Lauren, you just can't do that," Glory protested when Lauren first gently broached the subject. "Oh, I do thank you so much, but I couldn't. . . ." Her voice trailed off, but her eyes spoke volumes.

"It's something I want to do." Lauren knew she could be as stubborn as anyone. Between customers, they did manage to talk about the idea. At least Lauren managed to talk, over-riding Glory's protests firmly and, she told herself, commonsensibly.

And she did make some progress. Yes, Glory would talk to her parents; maybe just a loan? Maybe just for a semester or two, and then maybe she could get another scholarship or grant. "Maybe I can make my parents *think* about it," she said doubtfully from the kitchen door as she left. "I surely do thank you. It just seems like too much, though. Oh, Lauren!" She turned impetuously and threw her arms around Lauren, giving her a hug that made Lauren's heart sing.

Lauren watched her bike out to the road and sighed. The seed had been planted, and she hoped it would sprout. She couldn't mend

Glory's broken heart, but the girl's mind was certainly intact, and it would be a shame for her to miss college. . . .

Two hours later, after a long phone conversation with Glory's mother — who declared herself thunderstruck and certainly sounded that way — she thought there was a good chance the seed was germinating. She still had some convincing to do, she knew.

But still she felt hopeful. And when Perry called shortly after six, she told him she thought it just might work. "If only the Mitchells will trust me and not think I have some kind of ulterior motive," she added. "I'd feel so good about doing it."

"You're wonderful, and I love you," he told her, and she glowed — a glow that dimmed just slightly when he told her he couldn't stop by that evening.

Something about an old client of his and a will change. He seemed genuinely sorry, but she found herself biting her lip as she hung up, disappointed. Was marrying a country lawyer like marrying an old-fashioned country doctor who made house calls?

Still, he hadn't asked her to marry him yet, had he? Just what *was* it in his past that he wanted to talk about?

It hadn't taken Perry as long as he'd feared

t might to take care of Joseph Morrison's current problems. If the curmudgeonly old goat hadn't been a longtime friend of the family as well as a client, he'd never have gone to see him rather than Lauren.

He glanced at his watch. Maybe he could stop by and surprise Lauren — but no, there was something else he really ought to do. Call George Mitchell, whom he'd known for a long time, and talk to him about Lauren's offer to help Glory. He and George respected each other, and maybe he could overcome any objection . . . though they'd think, of course, that he was speaking as a disinterested observer, and disinterest didn't enter into it at all.

Leaning back in his chair after talking to George, he smiled. He thought he'd opened the door a crack, perhaps. The smile grew as he looked at the coffeepot on his file cabinets. Move that, and the steamboat model at Country Blues would fit just perfectly.

Just as perfectly as Lauren fit into his arms and was going to fit into his life, once she understood — and she'd surely understand, wouldn't she? — the persistent ghost of the past that just wouldn't quite leave him alone. And just as she would fit into the life of Piney Ridge too. He had a little plan to help that along, one that he was sure would work.

He put it into operation first thing the nex morning.

His first stop was the pharmacy, where h picked up toothpaste and after-shave that h really didn't need.

"Didn't Glory Mitchell work here last sum mer?" he asked the woman at the registe when she rang up his purchases. "You know I heard something interesting yesterday. Confidentially, with a conspiratorial smile, h told her of Lauren's offer of help.

"Lauren Byrd? That California lady witl the antiques store? No kidding? Is that right! He could see her tucking the information in the back of her mind, slightly envious. Sh nodded, eyes bright, when he told her it wa a secret. "Won't say a thing yet, then," sh promised innocently.

"That's good." He could play the innocen as well as she could. "I'm not sure Miss Byrc wants it known yet. She's a bit shy, yo know."

"No! Now, who'd have thought *that?*"

A good start, he thought, and stopped b: the hardware store for an assortment o screws, mollie bolts, and short lengths o shelving — which he did need. "Outgrowin; my office," he told Carl Clemmens. "An Lauren Byrd, out there at Country Blue: needs a couple of display shelves. Though

I'd help her out."

"That so?" Carl Clemmens shot a sideways glance at Perry, half assessing. "Good-looking woman, she is, Perry. Better watch out. Handsome is as handsome does, my mama always said."

"Well," he drawled, "I know your mama was right about a lot of things. In this case, handsome *does* pretty well too." And he passed on the choice bit of information about Lauren's generosity.

"Hmph!" Carl seemed to be turning Perry's news over in his mind, as if he were looking for a booby trap among the posies. At last he gave Perry a small wondering shake of the head, his change, and a thoughtful look. "Hmph! Is that right, now?"

Back in the car, Perry considered the situation for a few moments before he started off again. He'd probably done enough for now. He smiled and headed to the office to do some paperwork.

By four he was ready to take a break. Besides, it was time to find out how well his scheme was working.

He slipped into a small window booth at the café and told Liz he was perishing for a cup of her terrific coffee. She beamed at him and told him that the apple pie was terrific today too, so he beamed back and said he'd just check that out, thanks.

It didn't take him long to find out what he wanted to know; it was served up to him right along with the pie and coffee. "You know that young woman you were with that day it rained so hard? Laura or Lorrie or whatever, the one with the antiques store?"

He assured her that he knew Lauren well, and what about her?

"Darnedest thing. Can't tell a book by its cover, can you?"

He shook his head, patient. These things took time.

"Well, she must be pretty nice. Some of these city people move in and think they're better than folks who've lived here all their lives, you know? Not you, of course — you've sort of been here, off and on, all your life."

He shook his head again, still patient, and then decided he should change the shake to a nod.

"Know what she's doing?" Perry looked expectant, and Liz leaned over and lowered her voice. "I heard she's sending Glory off to college — paying for it all — and graduate school too, if she wants it, and maybe even a new car. Can you beat that?"

Perry stifled a laugh and tried to look suitably impressed. It was a moment before he could trust his voice.

"Is that right?" he asked with the perfect note of wonder in his voice. The gossip machine was well oiled and operating just as smoothly as he had hoped. When the rumors had quieted and the wheat had been separated from the chaff, people would find themselves thinking of Lauren in a different way. "Now, is that *right?*" he repeated and grinned up at Liz.

Thursday was a very good day at Country Blues, from a business standpoint. Summer people decorating new cottages or refurbishing in country style stopped by. Buyers, not browsers. Lauren sold a Hoosier cupboard, a set of pine chairs, a chest of drawers, and a number of small decorative items. But her mind was on the next night, when Perry would fix dinner and she'd know the whole truth and nothing but the truth, so help you, Attorney Lucas. She felt apprehensive, a little fluttery (*Me! Of all people!* she scolded herself), and very, very happy. She watched Glory wrap a tole tray — poised, serious, mature — and wondered which of the two of them felt more like a lovestruck calf.

Pops called at two, an odd note in his voice. His drawl seemed to have evaporated like mountain mist on a summer day. "The mail just came," he told her. "I think you should see this. Busy?"

"Come on by," she answered. "I can always make time for you. What's it all about?"

"You'll see."

He was there within fifteen minutes, his eyebrows fairly bristling with what seemed to be a combination of amusement and indignation. "Here," he said, thrusting an envelope at her. "Take a look at this. From the Peabody creature."

It took her a few minutes to digest the contents of the letter. And the contract attached to the letter. And the ramifications, direct and indirect, of the whole situation.

"A gallery show in Chicago! Why, Pops, that's wonderful!"

"But note how she tried — oh, so cleverly — to leave Miss Lauren Byrd out of the whole thing. Making tentative hints that she'd rather deal direct with me, rather than through Country Blues."

"That's all right with me, Pops — I'm just so happy for you."

"I know that, honey, but you see what she's doing, don't you? She figures she can get a bigger cut of any sales for herself if she eliminates you as a middleman — excuse it, middlewoman. Anyway, she thinks she's dealing with a country bumpkin, I think. And she's going to be surprised. I spent a great deal of my life dealing with sharpies like Miz Peabody. I'll write up an alternate contract that'll make her penciled eyebrows fall off."

Lauren looked at Pops's sparking eyes and his squared shoulders and chuckled. "I believe it, Mr. Carmichael." She glanced down at the envelope. "Um, Mr. T. P. Carmichael, is it? Who spent his life dealing with 'sharpies'? Mr. C., I have a personal question I hope you won't mind my asking. I really think I've known you long enough to be nosy."

"You have two of them, I expect," Pops said resignedly. "What kind of business I was in back there in Michigan before I moved to Piney Ridge. And what T. P. stands for." He stopped.

He looked unhappy, but she wasn't going to let him off the hook. "Confession is good for the soul," she assured him.

"Bah. But all right. I was, for nearly forty years, a state senator. An honest one too, though I've done my share of wheeling and dealing, and I had a reputation as a tough cookie."

"I'll bet you did — that you were —" Lauren was at a loss for words. So here was the real Pops Carmichael. "My goodness," she said at last, a bit weakly.

"After that, you still want to hear about my name?"

She nodded, mute. Glory had appeared in the kitchen door, listening. Charlie flicked an ear, staring at Pops.

"Throckmorton Poindexter Carmichael. My mother's grandfather was a judge, way back, and it was his name. Mama was proud of him and wanted me to be just like him. Instead, I spent my life living down a ridiculously grandiose appellation."

"No easy task," Lauren agreed gravely.

"Especially for a Seabee in the Pacific during the war," he assured her. "Tough one too. Started to go by the name Mort then, and it stuck. But when I moved down here, I just told everyone to call me Pops. They did and you did."

"And I expect Penelope Peabody will too." She chortled. "Your real name just doesn't sound like a backwoods primitive artist. 'Pops' sounds better for promotional purposes."

"True." He took the letter and contract back from her and stared down at it thoughtfully. "I'm touched, though. Really." There was a confusing mixture of pride and humility in his eyes, and Lauren hugged him.

"You deserve it. But I just wonder what other secrets you have buried in that deceitful heart of yours, you old fraud!"

The gently sad look on his face intensified. "More than you know, honey. One of these days we'll sit down and I'll tell you tales . . . but not right now." He bent to kiss Lauren on the forehead, bent further to scratch Charlie behind the ear, and waved a hand at a gaping Glory.

"Have to work hard to be ready for my own show, you know!" he called back at them as he left. A pleased smile had returned to light his eyes, and his eyebrows and moustache nearly vibrated with electricity. "Isn't this old world just full of surprises!"

Glory, Lauren, and Charlie stared at the screen door for several long seconds. Glory was the first to find her voice.

"It surely is, isn't it?" she said wonderingly. "Throckmorton Poindexter Carmichael? I like Pops better."

Lauren nodded soberly in agreement and wondered just what secret Pops was hinting at. All of a sudden it seemed that everyone was on the verge of telling her his secrets. If the world were any more full of surprises, she feared for her sanity.

Chicken Kiev on a bed of rice and salad, Perry decided. He'd done it once before, and it had worked pretty well, though he wasn't much of a chef. Croissants from the bakery downtown, since he wasn't a miracle worker. And a good bottle of Riesling. . . .

He put his silver candleholders — from the SS *Cleopatra* — on the table. Great. This part was easy. And he fully intended to ask her to marry him, and that wouldn't be difficult. He'd been rehearsing exactly what he would say for the past three days.

The difficult part would be the part that he'd decided to schedule for over the after-dinner coffee. True Confessions, he'd labeled it in his mind. And he'd rehearsed all that too. He was sure she loved him. There was certainly no doubt in his mind that he loved her. He'd convince her with perfect judicial logic that he was a good man. Now if only he could convince himself. . . .

Perhaps, he fantasized as he coated the chicken rolls and checked the temperature of the wine, she'd show up at the door in a glorious chiffon caftan — sea green, maybe, to float sensuously about her. Or — no, flame-colored, like a fire in the soul.

The pleasant reverie gave way to reality when she arrived — wearing an attractive but practical pale-blue skirt and soft blouse and the sweetest smile he'd ever seen. "Something wrong?" she asked after a moment, smile fading. He realized he'd been staring, memorizing her just as she was — perfectly beautiful.

"Just admiring," he said.

Her smile returned. "Well, thank you. I

brought a lemon meringue pie. Lily Mae made it and brought it by this afternoon." Her smile was slightly anxious. "You're all right?"

"Just admiring," he repeated and then caught himself. What had happened to his self-assurance, anyway? He wanted to lean forward and kiss her, but he'd have to lean into the meringue. He took the pie from her and led the way to the kitchen.

"Thank you, Lily Mae," he said to their absent benefactor, putting the pie carefully on the counter and taking a deep breath. And then — was it his idea or Lauren's? — they were working together companionably at the kitchen counter, touching lightly now and then and smiling at each other. Lauren made the salad and took the wine to his small dining room, with its steamboat dining table and heavy upholstered chairs. She lit the candles, and their glow made her eyes shine luminously. Lauren was beside him, helping him as if she had always done so, and the physical and emotional warmth of that fact was almost unbearably wonderful.

Still, she kept stealing glances at him, a question deep in her eyes, but she asked no questions. He was grateful for that.

"To us," he toasted her over the wine-glasses. She echoed his words, but the questioning look deepened. "We'll have coffee and a long talk after dinner in the living room," he told her.

Nodding, she gave him a long, level look. Then she smiled and told him — sincerely, he thought — that he made the best chicken Kiev she'd ever eaten.

"I'll give you the recipe," he offered, pleased.

"Please don't. I'd rather just let you be the Kiev maker in the family," she said, and a flush spread across her cheeks as she realized what she'd intimated.

He told her he liked that idea, and the flush faded.

She told him about Pops's letter and the possibility of a show. And about Pops's background and his name. He was surprised, but it answered questions he'd had in his own mind. It was perfect small talk, so light and optimistic, so upbeat.

So why, as they lingered over the fluffy sweet-tartness of Lily Mae's pie, did he feel nervous? Fragments of his rehearsed speech went through his mind, fell into meaningless phrases like bits of last year's confetti. And Lauren had that darned questioning look back in her eyes again.

"I'm going to settle you in the living room with a cup of my best gourmet coffee, start up my new Vivaldi CD, and spirit these dishes into the kitchen sink," he told her.

"I'll help."

"No, you won't. Not this time. You'll sit back and relax."

"Please don't worry," she said unexpectedly.

She couldn't have explained why she said that. All evening the conversation had been pleasant, cheerful, bright. But under it, she'd sensed his growing tension. And when he joined her on the deep, squishy comfort of the living-room sofa, she had worked herself into a state of tension that nearly matched his.

He started haltingly, staring into a coffee cup he held clutched tightly in both hands as if it were a life preserver. "It's a little like the — what was their name, the Lees? Not a nice story." Head still lowered, he glanced up at her, eyes full of remembered pain. Voice low, he told her about working and grieving and drinking too hard. Barely aware that she had moved closer to him, that her hand was on his arm, he told her almost tonelessly about the unidentifiable face that haunted him. . . .

"I remember hitting him. I remember him going down the embankment — without a sound — and I blank out all the rest."

"Perry," Lauren said, beginning to understand, "listen to me." She put her cup on the coffee table and turned toward him, grasping his arms and trying to turn him toward her. He wouldn't meet her eyes. "Perry, you don't even remember what started the fight. Maybe he provoked it. And probably he was all right."

"I've heard all that before. But what I remember best was the fury — a red-hazed rage and a feeling that I really wanted to kill the man. And maybe I did just that. So I'm left with this — this ghost and a fear of what I might be capable of. . . ."

"Ghosts can be exorcised," she told him softly. "It just isn't in you to kill anyone. You're *not* like John Lee. I never should have mentioned him, should I?" Ruefully she raised her hands to either side of his face and looked into those shadowed eyes. "I love you, Perry. Your story doesn't change that."

He met her eyes then, and she could see the shadows thinning and lifting. Replaced by something else, something that flowed between the two of them like the surge of floodwaters too long dammed up. He made an inarticulate noise deep in his throat and pulled her into his arms, and she let herself drown.

Charlie greeted her exuberantly when she floated back to Country Blues. "Floated" was the right word for it, she supposed.

But she came down to earth with a heart-stopping thump as she reached the bottom of her back stairs.

A couple of storage boxes were there — linens in one, small unpriced items in the other.

And she could swear she hadn't left them partially obstructing the bottom step like that. Yet of course she must have; she was just being paranoid again. No one could have been in Country Blues — because Charlie was in the house the whole time she was gone, and Charlie wouldn't have allowed anyone in.

Still, it was a reminder that she hadn't changed the locks. She growled aloud at herself in exasperation. Some of that wonderful floating glow had dimmed just a tiny bit, and she hated to lose even an atom of it.

Chapter Thirteen

Perry padded down the stairs barefooted, wrapped in his dark-blue terry robe, and put the coffee on. Eight o'clock already. What was she doing now? He reached for the phone to find out, but it shrilled at him with an incoming call before he could pick up the receiver. There she was. A wave of happiness and longing swept over him, and he snatched the phone up eagerly.

"Good morning, beautiful," he crooned to it.

"I don't think I'm who you think," said Joe Reilly's voice, somewhat confusingly, from the other end. "You all right, Perry? Yeah, I guess you are." There was a hint of laughter in the last words. "I won't ask who she is, but I'm glad she's so beautiful."

"Oh," Perry said, acutely deflated. "Joe. Sorry."

"Don't be. Not yet, anyway. I have some information that's — well, kind of interesting." His voice faltered a little bit.

Perry felt his neck and shoulder muscles tighten, and a shadow fell over the bright morning. "What is it, Joe?"

"Bones, Perry. Found yesterday by an angler down near Festus. Time and the river didn't leave much but bones. Normally I'd have paid no heed, not my immediate concern, but —"

"But?"

"Oldish bones — been in the river maybe two or three years, the pathologist says. Height and age kind of correspond with your story. No identification. One item on the report that caught my eye. Probably doesn't mean a thing, you understand — but which side did you say that gold tooth was on?"

"Upper right, near the front," Perry answered. A chill spread glacially over his mind. He waited for a moment, but there was only silence on the other end of the line. "Joe?"

"Yeah, that corresponds. Okay, the police artist is going to do a drawing, a reconstruction. Want me to send you a copy of it? Just to satisfy your mind that this isn't the guy, of course."

"Of course," Perry repeated automatically. "I mean — no." He was thinking very fast. Adrenaline had chased away the last of the languor. "Don't send it — I'm driving up today, anyway." That hadn't been on his agenda, but something, a kind of instinctive inner voice, was taking over his plans. "I'll come in."

"All right, then. Listen, friend, this is probably a false alarm. But I'll be here all day. Just don't worry, okay?"

"I'll try. See you, Joe."

He let his breath out in a low, thoughtful whistle as he put the telephone down. Wildly racing thoughts made his head whirl. Yet the icy jab of uncertainty about the skeletal remains in St. Louis were more than compensated for by the warm knowledge that Lauren knew and understood and loved. . . .

He wished she could drive up with him. For moral support and because he wanted to show her off to his parents, his aunts and uncles and cousins by the dozens — but it was Saturday, a bad day for her to get away on short notice. But maybe?

No, she said when he called, with such regret in her voice that it seemed necessary to spend several minutes assuring each other that everything would be all right. She'd be thinking of him every minute, she said. She seemed to be on the verge of telling him something else, but then said it was nothing important.

A feeling of wary happiness settled across his shoulders by the time he was started on his way up the highway. This trip might clear up some questions. And he'd come back and take up a new life, install an alarm system at Country Blues, and. . . .

It was three in the afternoon when he walked into Joe Reilly's office. Joe looked at him searchingly after a brief greeting, then, without comment, handed him a slim manila folder. Perry was acutely conscious of the thumping of his heart. He felt a slight tremor in his hands as he opened the folder.

And then — a mixture of relief and disappointment. "The jury's still out, I think," he told Joe. "This isn't even close."

"Of course, it's just an approximation," Joe warned him. "At best, we can only guess at some things."

"I know that." Perry slapped the folder down and sat back in his chair. "This poor devil had a long, narrow face — that much is pretty clear. The face I remember had broad cheekbones, a low, wide forehead, and a much more protuberant jaw. Don't feel bad, though, Joe — the tooth is right."

"I tried." Joe made the words slightly plaintive. "Honest, I tried. Hoped we could settle this once and for all, get the ghoulies and ghosties out of your mind one way or the other."

"Thanks, Joe." Perry gave him a lopsided grin. "But maybe I'm finally getting some perspective about the whole thing. I'd still like to know, but it doesn't drag me down the way it did."

"Aha!" Joe looked pleased. "That new love bringing blessings to your life, is she? About time. You'll be bringing her by one of these days?"

"I will." The two men exchanged the long, understanding look of men who'd long been friends. "But you have to promise to keep all your blarney and Irish charm to yourself. She wouldn't be taken in by any of it, anyway, and besides, she's all mine."

Joe pushed his chair back, hoisted his feet to his desk and his eyebrows to his hairline. "Ah, the pity of it," he said with mock resignation.

Perry's father was in Chicago on a business trip, his mother told him when he called, and then, predictably, added, "What on earth have you been doing with yourself? Why haven't you been by? At least you could call."

"I did call last week, Mom," Perry protested. "And I've been busy. But I think I have some interesting news for you."

"You've *met* someone." She imbued the word "met" with a world of meaning, intuitively picking up the vibrations of good news. "Oh, my dear. Now, come by for dinner. The Historical Preservation Association will be here for the annual potluck, so there'll be lots of food, and they'll want to hear about her —"

"I doubt that," he answered wryly, cutting her off. Briefly he confirmed her guess at his news. "I'll bring her by as soon as possible, Mom. But I'll skip the potluck." Not that he had anything against the Historical Preservation Association, except that there were times when he thought they made heavy going of what should be thoroughly enjoyable projects.

"George Perkins is giving a talk on local Indian tribes," she told him, as if this would make it impossible for him to refuse.

That cinched it. George Perkins was a pompous windbag. "Mmm. Well, I promised Aunt Margaret I'd stop by this trip." Not quite the truth, but close enough. His great-aunt had been exceedingly hurt when he hadn't come to see her on his last trip.

"Oh. Well, I suppose." His mother's voice cooled. Aunt Margaret was his father's side of the family, something of a ditherer and not one of her favorite people. "Just as long as you promise to bring this Lauren — what did you say her last name was, Byrd? A Virginia Byrd, do you think? We had a family connection back about four generations ago, you know."

He stopped her before she could climb into

243

the tangled branches of the genealogical tree. "I have no idea what species of Byrd she is," he said and finally managed to hang up.

Aunt Margaret was delighted to hear from him. She'd pop a casserole into the oven and bake those beaten biscuits he loved, and would he like cole slaw? He assured her he would, and an hour later was settled into one of her soft, cushy chintz armchairs.

He accepted the obligatory "small spot of sherry" and watched, amused, as she downed hers in one long, though ladylike, gesture, re-filling her glass immediately from the cut glass decanter that sat on the rosewood table beside her. She'd linger over this one, just as she always had, while talking nonstop. Eighty-one years sat upon her shoulders like thistledown. She was as active now as she'd been when he'd been a small boy.

He'd always felt particularly close to Aunt Margaret, and so he told her about Lauren. She glowed and poured another sherry for both of them, saying wistfully that she wished that Uncle Delbert were alive to see this day. She fed him abundantly and patted his arm and drifted into familiar paths of conversation.

Which, this time, included a cruise to Jamaica.

"I'd planned on Europe this year, except

hat, as you know, some of my investments haven't been quite as profitable as I'd hoped. But perhaps next year."

He nodded, only half paying attention to her familiar words. She'd invested some of the money Uncle Delbert had left her in Clovis Properties, Inc., and was one of those who'd lost a bundle in the process. Perry's mind wandered off on that track, his hard work on the case, his frustration at hitting a brick wall. It was one of those threads in life that are sometimes left dangling. . . .

"The auction was terribly packed," she was saying. "I went because I thought maybe I could pick something up really cheap, get even with the man by practically stealing one of his treasures. But nothing good was left. I should have known."

"Sorry," Perry said, jerked back to the present. "Whose — which auction? I missed part of that."

"Why, the Jacoby auction, of course. Mr. Jacoby was a partner or something of Clovis's, wasn't he? Of course he was; I distinctly remember it. He died two months ago, quite unexpectedly. And there were dealers and wholesalers there from all over, and some very disreputable-looking gentlemen — No, not gentlemen — they looked more like gangsters. Anyway, they were pushing around, looking over things like a flock of vultures."

"Tom Jacoby died?" Perry still wasn't sure he'd heard right.

"That's what I just said, isn't it? Probably died of meanness and avarice. Can one die of avarice? I'm sure one can die of meanness. Like my Uncle Bartholomew did."

"Aunt Margaret." He touched her arm, trying to halt the flow of words. "Back up a minute. I hadn't heard about Tom Jacoby's death." Little pieces were clicking together in his mind. It couldn't be. Those pieces *couldn't* fit together in just that way.

"Why not?" he asked aloud, bringing a puzzled look to his great-aunt's face.

"You mean why hadn't you heard of Tom Jacoby's death, dear?"

"No, not that, but connected. Tell me about those gangster types and all you remember of who bought what. Everything."

Gently, but with a number of inevitable unprofitable detours, he picked his aunt's remarkably retentive memory of the auction. Her description of the two men who bought the majority of the trunks of papers and odds and ends was vivid. Perry had little doubt when she'd finished: It had been Dutch and Harry.

It was hard to believe that anything incriminating had been left among the papers at

Jacoby's death. Still, it had been a sudden death. Still, "vultures" had gathered at the auction — his aunt's intuition was excellent. So there was something. . . .

"But what does it mean?" she asked, looking perplexed.

"I'm not sure, but if I'm right, I'll explain it all one of these days," he told her. Right now he wanted to call Lauren. She would have one answer he needed. He managed to escape from Aunt Margaret only after promising that he'd bring Lauren to see her soon and that he'd keep her informed of "anything interesting in the case of that rotten, predatory old buzzard, rest his soul."

He'd always thought she had a refreshingly honest way of looking at people and events. Lauren would love her.

It was a busy Saturday, but Lauren's mind kept straying — to thoughts of Perry, of the evening before, of what he might be finding out in St. Louis. He couldn't bring the man back to life, even if he'd killed him. Which she didn't believe. But maybe it was terribly important to Perry to *know*. She was glad Glory was here to help out; her mind felt like an overstretched rubber band.

Jake phoned about midafternoon, saying he'd be in town first thing Monday morning.

"I carved a whole new set of animals," he said. "Have to be at the dentist at eight-thirty, but I could bring them by your place early, if you'd like to see them."

It was a perfect diversion from her thoughts of Perry. Her antennae quivered, and her mind snapped to attention. "An ark, Jake," she said excitedly. "How about a Noah's Ark? Lots of work, but it would be profitable. Think about it, and I'll see you Monday." Bless Perry for having introduced her to Jake!

Perry. The diversion was over. What had he learned? The suspense was terrible, and she felt so far away from him. . . .

When the phone rang at last just before eight, she nearly jumped out of her skin. She'd hardly eaten any dinner. She'd paced the house, with Charlie trotting so close at her heels that she almost screamed at him. The rubber band was stretching dangerously thin. And Perry's first unromantic words didn't help.

"Did Dutch and Harry mention the name of the man who'd owned the stuff they bought at auction?" he asked without preamble, voice tense with suppressed excitement. "Where are they now? Can we get hold of them? Are they in the area?"

"I love you too," she told him sweetly.

'Though I try not to let it show too much, unlike you."

There was a throaty chuckle. "Sorry, my sweet. I promise I'll make up for this later. But I learned something that might explain your prowlers and might tie into a case I was working on. Look, I'll explain it all when I get there, early tomorrow."

"Apology accepted. The answer to your question is that I can't remember any specific name, but I think I can find out where Dutch and Harry are. Do you want me to try?"

"Please. They may know something very important."

"Perry? What about —" She hesitated. "What about the body?"

"Body? Oh, that. It wasn't him. Is that good or bad?"

"I wish I knew, and I wish you knew too."

"Yes. . . . " His voice faded briefly. "Maybe someday. But now it just seems that there are more important things — like you, like finding out who's been sneaking into Country Blues and why."

And who had apparently done it again, last night, she thought with a shiver. "Hurry back," she said softly. "Please."

Lauren spent the greater part of Sunday morning alternately clock watching — how soon would Perry be back, anyway? — and trying in vain to find out where Dutch and Harry might be.

Most of the antiques shops scattered across the southern part of the state were closed, and there was no answer. And of the two where she received an answer, she learned nothing. No, they didn't know where Dutch and Harry might be this weekend. They'd been through last week or the week before. She might try. . . .

She tried, feeling more and more frustrated.

Perry's car pulled into her driveway just as she was flipping her sign to Open, and she quickly reversed it back to Closed. Sunday might be a good afternoon for customers, but today they were unimportant. They could wait until some other day, darn it.

He burst through her back door like a tornado, whirling her up off her feet and giving her no chance at all to say anything whatsoever. Which was, she thought — insofar as she could think — as it should be. It was several minutes before she could catch her breath, and even then, she wasn't sure she wanted to.

It was Perry who finally pulled away, took a deep breath, and managed to speak semicoherently. "Dutch and Harry," he said.

"Have you found them? It could be important."

"*That* important?"

He hesitated for a moment and then drew her to him again. "Not as important as you." He kissed her slowly, lingeringly. "But it could be *very* important," he said when he paused to draw breath. "I can't be sure. There could have been something in what Dutch and Harry brought you that could put you in a certain amount of danger. If someone wants it badly enough."

And maybe someone *had* been skulking around Country Blues again two nights ago. She swallowed and tried to think rationally.

"But we went through all of it —"

"Maybe we did, and maybe we didn't. If we can get hold of Dutch and Harry, we can verify just where everything came from. There might even be a possibility that they'd remember something that would help us. Something we've overlooked."

Her overwhelming curiosity was making her feel just a bit exasperated. Couldn't he start at the beginning and explain this thing carefully? But when she suggested that he do just that, Perry opened his mouth, closed it again, and then shook his head.

"Not right this minute — it's much too long a story. Isn't there somewhere you can call,

251

try to trace them down?"

Some of his intensity was rubbing off o her. And a tiny needle of fear was beginnin to prick at the edges of her mind. *Could* sh be in any danger? Surely not. Yet. . . . "Ther are a few more places I can try, and I ca call back some that didn't answer earlier. Jus keep your fingers crossed."

He crossed them well, apparently. On th third call she reached Annie's Attic over i Plainfield.

"Dutch and Harry? They were here yes terday," Annie said. "Heading for, um, Birc Bluff, I think. That help?"

"That helps. Thanks." She hung up an stood chewing at her bottom lip. Birch Bluf — not that far away.

"Well?" Perry almost exploded behind her "Where are they?"

"Birch Bluff." She was talking to hersel as much as to him. "I remember when the headed there once before when they left here Harry said they liked to camp out over tha way when the weather was nice. Birch Grov Park? Does that sound right?"

"It does. Grab your sunglasses, woman — we're going to take a chance. Thirty miles Maybe twenty minutes."

"Good heavens, I hope not," she groaned But she was right behind him as he raced dow

he back steps — pausing only to make doubly
ure, this time, that her door was securely
ocked behind her. And Charlie could stay
ight there on the porch while they were gone
— if that was any deterrent at all.

Lauren was grateful that Perry's ETA was
xaggerated, though he didn't exactly waste
ime. As the car roared over the winding roads,
e told her of the Clovis case, its growth from
local scandal to a Federal case — and of
is own frustrations.

"And someone, it seems, didn't like it at
ll that something — probably something
ncriminating — might have made it to the
uction house. Did Dutch and Harry ever
nention the name Jacoby to you?"

They hadn't, as far as she could remember.
But surely they'd soon find out — if they were
ucky enough to find Dutch and Harry.

They were. The White Elephant, as Harry
ometimes called his truck, was parked at the
orth edge of Birch Grove Park. A few feet
rom it, lolling comfortably beside a brick fire
it, were the two men — who looked aston-
shed at the sudden appearance of Perry and
he "purtiest antiques dealer in their terri-
ory." Who listened, nodded, and said — at
east Harry did — that yep, that's right, it
vas the Jacoby auction, and what was this all
n aid of, anyhow? And listened some more

and nodded again.

"Well, now, who'd have thought it?" Harry said. "We can't have our Lauren Byrd in hot water, can we? Hey, Dutch, wasn't it that ratty old Gladstone bag?"

"It was," Dutch replied solemnly, his eyebrows almost meeting in a spot directly above his nose as he frowned in recollection.

"There was a bunch of stuff in there, didn't make no sense to me, but I figured Lauren could throw it out, if she wanted," Harry explained to Perry. "Looked like computer printouts, nothing I could make heads or tails out of. Suppose that could be it?"

"That old Gladstone. I remember it." Lauren's face reflected Dutch's frown. "But it only had an assortment of old hanks of yarn in it. I didn't even empty it all the way."

"Well, there you are, then," Harry said triumphantly. "If you haven't found anything else in all your looking, then what you haven't found has to be where you didn't look, isn't that right?" Confusing as the question was, there was logic in it. Lauren nodded and looked at Perry, who appeared to be ready to sprint back to the car again.

Harry grinned. "While you're here, want to see the old kitchen table and chairs we picked up yesterday at a farm sale? Thought of you when I got them."

"Not now," Perry said, but Lauren laid a
and on his arm.

"Two minutes. Let me look." Her antennae
were quivering again, and what difference
would two minutes make?

Perry rolled his eyes heavenward. "Suppose
might as well get used to it," he growled,
nd Harry stared at him.

"Like that, is it?" he said with smug sat-
sfaction. "Couldn't happen to two nicer peo-
le. Now I remember a few years back when
met this nice widder woman down near the
tate line —"

"I'll just take a fast look," Lauren inter-
upted quickly. No sense in pushing Perry's
patience too far, after all.

And the chestnut table and chairs, she de-
ided as soon as she saw them, were just what
he needed — if she could get them to Piney
Ridge. They certainly wouldn't fit in Perry's
ar.

"Shoot, we'll follow you back — no prob-
em," Harry offered. "For a beer, maybe?"
And within a few minutes they were back on
he road, the pickers' truck lumbering along
behind them like a snorting rhinoceros.

"You're the most remarkable —" Perry
began, and then laughed. "All right. You
know where the bag is?"

"I know. Hurry." Obviously he was hur-

rying. She clenched hands that were itchin
to get into that bag again. . . .

She'd dragged the shabby old Gladstone u
to the kitchen table by the time Dutch an
Harry got there. Hanks and balls of faded yar
littered the tablecloth, along with crumple
computer paper that Perry was studying wit
a ferocious scowl.

"Find what you're looking for, and sha
I put the table and chairs on the back porch?
Harry called in.

"Yes, I think, to both questions." Sh
popped the tops of a couple of cans of bee
and handed them out the door.

But Perry's face looked blankly disap
pointed. There was nothing obvious in the pa
pers, then. She sighed and listened to th
thumping and bumping as Dutch and Harr
moved the table from the truck. Lauren wrot
out a check and walked out onto the porch
feeling Perry's disappointment in her ow
heart. "It was nice of you to bring it all th
way back," she told Harry, but he shrugge
away her thanks.

"I was sort of thinking about coming bac
this way anyhow. There's a nice lady tend
bar down at the Watering Trough I though
I'd like to go see. Coming, Dutch?"

"Well, no," Dutch said slowly, looking fron

Perry to Lauren to Harry. "Tell you what. I'll drop you off there, and you can have your brew in peace, like, and I'll take the truck on up and see what Lily Mae needs in the way of canning jars and such." Lauren had never before heard him utter such a long statement.

"But, Dutch — we ain't got no canning jars this trip!"

Dutch grinned, a silly grin that almost reached his ears and wreathed his weathered cheeks in a thousand fine lines. "Now, Harry, I know that," he said, and turned and walked out the door.

Harry stood looking after him, astonishment leaving him gape-jawed. "Well, I'll be a flat-footed, pointy-nosed, odiferous woods kitty," he finally managed. And then, for the first time that Lauren could remember, words seemed to fail him.

Chapter Fourteen

Lauren watched the big white truck puff its elephantine way down the driveway and turned back to Perry. "Nothing?" she asked.

"Not a thing. Yet. Still, someone apparently wants it. Come here." She did, expecting him to show her a potentially meaningful line of figures or symbols, but instead he reached out and pulled her to him.

After a moment's silence, he said, "I don't like this."

"I do."

He chuckled, tightening his arms. "You know what I mean. If these papers are as important as I suspect, they'll keep trying."

"Two nights ago —" She tried to swallow the little spark of uneasiness that was kin to fear. "I — I had the feeling someone had been here. Could have been imagination."

His arms tightened even more, protectively, almost convulsively, and he made a growling sound deep in his throat.

"You're squishing," she protested.

"Sorry. But not very. Let's get you packed."

"Get me *packed?*"

"You and these papers are coming to my place. Now. I have an extra room, and I don't want you here alone."

"I have Charlie. And I don't like to leave the place vacant, open to whoever wants to come in."

"True." He looked thoughtful. "But for tonight, let's just take all the papers to my place. Leave Charlie on guard here, whatever good that does. And if we still don't find any answers, you may have to put up with a house guest. Me. Don't argue."

"Who's arguing?" Sometimes, she thought blissfully, no matter how good one might be at taking care of one's self, it was wonderful to have someone — the right someone — to lean on.

"It's settled, then. Get packed."

He was stowing her bag into his car when Charlie barked sharply, looking toward the road.

Lauren froze. Nels's Jag was pulling into her driveway. She really didn't want to see him right now. Not right now and not later, and maybe not ever. Nels and his insinuations, his brashness, his predatory instincts seemed to belong to a different world, now that she was in the circle of Perry's love.

Still, Nels had helped her with so many

little things when she'd first come to Piney Ridge. . . .

Nels seemed to sense the situation immediately. "Just came by for a little visit. Looks as if my timing's off. What's up?" He looked at them both assessingly.

Perry slammed the trunk lid shut. "She's coming to my place tonight." It was almost a challenge. "She's not safe here."

"Not safe?" Nels looked from one to the other. "What could be safer than a country antiques store?"

"She's had intruders. More than once." Perry's voice was curt. "Right now she shouldn't stay here alone."

"Maybe you're right." Nels stared at the ground, thoughtful. "Still, if no one's taken anything yet — they haven't, have they? — then why should they keep coming back?"

It was a logical enough question, Lauren thought. "Because," she started, "we think there might be —"

Perry cut her off with a warning glance. "Because we don't know what's going on, and it's better to play it safe."

"Of course." It was said laconically. "I see. Well, I'll come visit some other time, then."

"We'll be glad to see you," Perry said with exaggerated politeness. Nels didn't miss the slight stress on the "we," and his departure was accompanied by a rather excessive amount of wheel spinning and motor revving.

"So much for that," Lauren murmured. "I'll just lock up —" Then she stopped, listening. Through the diminishing roar of the Jag, she thought she could hear her telephone. "Back in a minute." She dashed back into the house, snatching the phone up breathlessly.

"Oh, my, Lauren, did I get you at a bad time? I'm sorry." Glory's voice was full of apology. "I just wanted to say I can come in real early tomorrow morning and do up those linens that need to be washed and starched, if that's all right. I have to be home before noon, but that should give me plenty of time."

Lauren took a deep breath. "Yes. That would be great, but I probably won't be here." She wondered how to explain that she'd be spending the night at Perry's.

"That's all right." Glory didn't question the statement at all. "I have my key, anyway, so I'll just come on in. You don't have to hurry back." As if she knew exactly where Lauren was going — and maybe she did. Maybe, already, the whole town did.

The last of the sunlight was fading when they pulled into Perry's drive. The house lay in twilight shadow, the spanking-white paintwork glimmering in the dusk.

"I like it," she said softly, and he turned off the ignition and put his hand over hers.

"It's yours," he said. "So am I. So is my family. So is my name, if you'll take it. Now — do I get the steamboat model?"

"Let me think." She lifted his hand to her lips, kissing the tips of one finger at a time. "I'm not exactly sure," she said judiciously. "If that's really a proposal, I believe something mutually advantageous could be worked out."

He leaned over and kissed her then, a thoroughly satisfying kiss. "I believe," he said after a moment, "that I have finally rectified any damage I did on our first meeting." And he kissed her again.

Perry stirred, turned, hovered in the no-man's-land at the edge of sleep. Something had awakened him. Was it a dream?

In the distance, thunder rumbled. Perhaps that was what had disturbed his sleep. A tentative breeze stirred the branches of the oak outside his window. There was a louder, slightly longer grumble of thunder. The fine weather was breaking.

But it wasn't just the thunder that had awakened him. He frowned, trying to concentrate. What were those whirling thoughts, dream ends, that were teasing at the edges of his mind?

Numbers. Numbers and symbols, code words.

Raising his head slightly, he glanced over at the clock. It was still only just after two. Strange how wide-awake he felt. And he felt on the verge of discovery of some sort. . . .

He tiptoed past Lauren's room, hoping he wouldn't awaken her. Downstairs, with a pot of coffee brewing to sharpen his wits and the windows open to catch the freshening breezes, he spread the papers from the old black bag over his kitchen table.

He found something — a reference, a sequence that seemed faintly familiar. He closed his eyes, trying to remember. Click. Yes, he'd seen it before — in the Clovis records. He unfolded the long printout, scanning columns, looking for repeats. Click. What he had learned during those long months of work back in St. Louis was being confirmed here, added to, supplemented.

Another row of figures, and a code name. Click. Almost, he had it — almost. There had to be something more.

A hand touched his shoulder softly, startling him. "It's thundering," came Lauren's sleepy voice. "It woke me up. I don't much like thunder." She paused, listening. "We don't have many electrical storms where I come from," she added apologetically.

He grasped her hand and turned to look up at her, standing there still full of sleep, wrapped haphazardly in a silky green kimono. He'd been so deeply engrossed in the papers before him, he hadn't realized that the weather had closed in on them. It wasn't a window-rattler, not yet, anyway, but the thunder was close, and the wind had risen to keen fretfully under the eaves.

"Just a lot of noise," he said soothingly. "But I'd better close the windows. Want a cup of coffee?"

"You do keep odd hours," she said, looking at the clock. The fog of sleep was clearing from her eyes. Pouring herself a cup of coffee, she looked at the muddle of papers on the table. "I have a rival for your affections, kind sir."

"No affection involved, dear lady. Just terrible curiosity."

"Find anything?"

He shrugged, his shoulders broad under the dark-blue robe. Lauren sat down with her coffee, looking at his shoulders, not at the papers. She wanted to lean her head against him, to be held while the thunder rumbled and the wind rose.

"I'm not sure." His mind seemed inextricably tangled in the computer printouts and the few small handwritten notes he'd found tucked in the folds. Somewhere, in the distance where he just couldn't quite get hold of it, he could hear those clicks of recognition — not quite of understanding. Not yet.

For the moment he gave it up. "I'm not sure of anything right now, except that I love you. Can't you come a little closer?"

She could and did, and neither of them heard the fury of the storm battering at the windows.

"Well. A lovely morning. Smells like rain here. How is it there?"

A curse. "Dark, that's what it is. Don't you ever sleep?"

"Not when there's work to be done. And you'd better wake up, because there's definitely work for you to do too."

"Come on. If none of us has found anything yet, there's nothing to be found. I thought we had agreed —"

"That was before Lionel had his little talk with the housekeeper last night. It took him a while to find her. She's retired and gone to live with her sister."

"All right, I'm awake and listening."

"There were dozens of shoe boxes in Jacoby's closet. There was also a box of yarn, old, she said, probably stashed away there by Jacoby's wife before she died five years ago. And there were papers crammed into some of the shoe boxes — possibly what we're looking for. But there was also an old case of some kind, a Gladstone, I think she called it."

"Go on."

"There were no near relatives to go through things, so the housekeeper did some cleaning out. Gave some stuff to charity, but thinks she just tossed the yarn and papers into the bag and set it aside, since the bag was old enough to be interesting and might sell at auction."

"And if it did, and if we're right about what those papers were, and if they should fall into Perry Lucas's hands —"

"Exactly. So, my friend, get there quickly. And find them."

"I think I may even have seen that bag — and this might be a good time to look."

"Call back as soon as you can. And don't mess up, got it?"

The rain dripping from the eaves woke Lauren in the morning. There was no rain, no thunder, no wind. The storm had passed.

The aroma of fresh-brewed coffee wafted up the stairs. Perry must be back at his deciphering again. Or was it still? She'd diverted him for a while last night, anyway, but she knew he'd gone back to those printouts after she returned to bed. She smiled and pulled on her robe. The coffee smelled wonderful.

In the kitchen, the dawn-dim light seemed to deepen the shadows around Perry's eyes. When he looked up at her, it was with the strangest expression — elation and sadness and love, all mixed. "Come in — sit down." His voice was strained.

"I'll make some breakfast."

"Not just now. You should hear this. It's not very pleasant, and I haven't figured it all out yet, but —"

He stopped, and she sat down, a little bewildered. Shouldn't he be happier that he'd found some answers? Why the strange look?

"This is too close to home, and I've known him all my life. It seems impossible, but it's there in black and white if you have the key, so it's possible, after all, isn't it?"

She let her fingertips graze the back of his hand. "I think possibly you'd better start at the beginning of all these possibilities, because you've lost me." Except that he hadn't, not entirely. A suspicion was beginning to form in her mind. . . .

"Yes. Sorry. Well, you already know part of it — about that frustrating Clovis case. I always thought there were others besides Jacoby and Clovis fiddling the books — in several states. And this" — he rustled the papers — "this proves it. There's enough for a case, not only against Clovis but against the second level of command — which includes a mutual acquaintance."

The suspicion became a near certainty, making her feel sad and disappointed. "Nels," she said softly. "Nels Hawke."

Perry nodded, murmuring that he was sorry. "So am I," she said. "But it figures. Lily Mae told me he'd made such an unexpected success of the resort after his father died — for reasons nobody suspected, I guess."

"He has a brother who seems to be involved."

"Lily Mae mentioned that too. In some kind of financial business, she said. Oh, Perry, I feel so stupid, so conned, so *used!* And Charlie was conned too. Charlie would have let Nels come into the shop — he was a friend. But wait. I was out with Nels during the first break-in. He couldn't have done it."

"He got you out of there, didn't he? For hours, so someone else could look, but they didn't have any luck. So Nels eventually did some looking on his own."

"Oh, Perry." She squeezed her eyes shut

in guilty remembrance. "When I first bought the shop, the plumbing went haywire. I was supposed to be at a sale in Clarkston that afternoon, and Nels stopped by and I gave him the key to the back door. He was so helpful — stayed and locked up after the plumber left — and I don't remember ever getting that key back."

"Mmm. You know, I wonder what he did last night. Maybe he went through the shop at leisure, since he knew you wouldn't be there."

She was on her feet in an instant, her face stricken.

"Now, love," he said, "it'll be all right. Justice will prevail."

"That's not the problem, my dear old barrister. I just realized it's after seven. It's not justice I'm worried about, it's Jake Mac-Nab, on his way to the dentist. And Glory and the linens. Don't look so confused — just get dressed and get me back to Country Blues." The words trailed behind her. She was already speeding on light, bare feet up the stairs.

Perry shook his head as if to clear it and obediently began to hurry. The first thing to do was get all those papers back into his office safe. At this point one couldn't be too careful.

★ ★ ★

They said little on the drive to Country Blues. Lauren glanced at her watch once or twice. Then, as they swung around the corner past the tiny church in its grove of trees two blocks from the shop, she craned her neck, looking back. "Odd," she said.

He looked in the rearview mirror. "What's odd?"

"Back there at the back of the parking lot. Under those low trees — it looked a little like Nels's car."

Perry's mouth tightened, and his foot pressed down on the accelerator, so that, when they pulled sharply into the driveway at Country Blues, the tires squealed in protest, and so did Lauren.

But she choked back her protest, glimpsing the wild tableau that presented itself in the field behind her back door.

Charlie galloped toward Perry's car at full speed and in full voice. Just behind him, waving her arms and mouthing words that couldn't be heard over the barking, came Glory. And behind that —

Sprawled face-down on the wet grass, his head turned away from them, was a man in dark rain gear. A fishing hat lay near him, as if it had flown from his head when he went down.

Which it probably had. On top of him, unconcernedly playing mumblety-peg and watching them approach, sat Jake MacNab.

It took three sharp commands before Charlie closed his mouth so that Lauren could hear either Jake or Glory, both of whom were in full spate. The figure on the ground didn't move. Lauren didn't care to look closely at him or need to. She knew who it was. Perry moved up to ask Jake a few quick questions. Lauren stood still, listening to Glory's tumbled, almost tearful words.

"It's all right now," Lauren told her, putting one arm around her shoulders. "Slow down. Tell me just what happened."

Glory gulped back an incipient sob. "I got here before seven. Thought I heard some noises — like from the cellar, you know? — but I decided it was just the water in the downspouts. Still, I had funny feelings inside, like Grandma gets —"

"Huh!" Jake interjected. "Funny ain't the word for it!"

"Anyway, Charlie came into the kitchen with me, and he didn't seem to think anything was wrong, so I went and got the box of linens. But I heard it again. A kind of" — she glanced toward Nels — "a kind of sneakin' sound. Scary. Oh, Lauren!"

"It's all right, Glory," Lauren repeated. Although it wasn't. It wasn't at all.

"Seemed as if it came from under the back porch. I took Charlie and snuck a peek out the door, and your old cellar door was moving. Up and down, like someone was trying to get it open."

Lauren looked over to the slanted wooden exterior doors. They stood open now, cellar steps sloping steeply away into the gloom. "They had a chain and padlock," she said.

"Yes, but there was an awful hard push from underneath, and I think a handle snapped." Glory gulped. "Then *he* came crawling out, hat pulled 'way down. I couldn't help it — I screamed."

"Like a banshee," Jake agreed. "I'd just pulled in the drive. Bloody murder, it sounded like. So I came a-runnin' —"

"Thank goodness!" Glory closed her eyes and took a deep breath. "Because by then he'd turned toward me, and I could see who it was and I couldn't figure out *why*. And he came toward me, looking so angry — and I screamed again."

"And I decided I'd better stop all these shenanigans, whatever they were, because it sure didn't look or sound very good. I just sorta flipped my knife, I did, and it caught him through the sleeve and pinned it to the porch post," Jake said.

"Just like in an old movie," Glory said with

admiration, smiling a little tremulously at Jake.

"Aw, 'twas easy," he said modestly. " 'Course, I had to come up quick while he was discombobulated and give him a good lick aside the jaw. That put him down where he is now." He looked down. "Who the heck is he, anyway, and what was he doing here?"

"That, Jake, is a long story," Perry said. "His name is Nels Hawke. And I think we'd better call the sheriff."

As if on cue, Nels got to his knees with a sudden, desperate lurch, throwing the small, older man off. Jake shook himself and turned to grasp at Nels's ankles, but speed and intensity born of fear propelled Nels toward the woods at the side of the property.

And Perry was right behind him. Nels was still groggy, and his desperation wasn't enough. With a flying tackle that took both of them tumbling through the grass, Perry took him down.

A deep, familiar anger raged through Perry — a red-hot fire that raced wildly along his veins. He pulled his arm back, ready to swing with all his strength, wanting to punish —

But then his arm dropped, and he sat back on his haunches, staring at the somewhat battered face of Nels Hawke.

"Just stay put, Hawke," he said, his voice

a little harsh with repressed emotion. "You're not going anywhere."

"Yeah." There was defeat in Nels's eyes as he glanced warily up at Perry. "Guess you know all about it, then."

There was a soft, cool hand at Perry's neck. "You know what you just did, Perry," Lauren murmured. "I know you do. You were in complete control. Now will you please believe in yourself?"

"With your help, I'll try." He scrambled to his feet as Nels began to move. "Don't push your luck, buddy," he said. "I can't guarantee that control."

"Not going anyplace," Nels mumbled. He looked from one to the other of them and brushed one muddy wet hand across his forehead, a hint of private pain in his eyes.

"A shame," he said to Lauren. "You know, I really could have cared about you. For the first time in my life I think I was falling in love. It all could have worked out. A shame." He sat quietly on the grass, shoulders slumped, staring blindly out at his own personal version of hell.

Epilogue

In the ensuing days, as the dust settled, there were plans to make — plans for a wedding, plans for their future together. They settled, tentatively, on possibly selling Lauren's place and moving Country Blues to a shop in a prime shopping area just off the main route. Lauren was blissful, Lily Mae and Glory beamed, and even Charlie smiled more than usual.

Perry had finally put his guilt over the unknown and unknowable past behind him. He was beginning to believe, as Lauren did, that somewhere out there, the man who had haunted his dreams was alive. Perhaps, at worst, he was still drifting and brawling along the waterfronts, though Perry hoped that he might have found a better life.

On a balmy afternoon, on the front porch of Country Blues, Lauren sat almost unbearably content on the refurbished 1920s porch glider she'd put out during the week. She was flanked by the two men who meant so much to her — Perry and Pops. Charlie lay, head on paws, carefully equidistant from what he apparently regarded as "his people," where he could keep a sleepy eye on all three.

"It just doesn't get much better than this." She meant it from the bottom of her heart. "Champagne," she said, getting up and stretching luxuriously. "That's what we need. But I don't have any. I think there's some zinfandel, though, and I feel this unsquelchable need to make a toast to a future full of sunshine and promise."

"Sit down." Pops put a hand on her arm as she started to walk inside. "Because, speaking of promises, I've got a speech to make too. Seems like maybe this just might be a good time."

Lauren sat down, looking a little anxiously at Pops. He looked so serious, slightly uncertain.

"Promises," he said. "They can be hard to keep sometimes, seems like, but some keep them only too well." He paused to take a deep breath. "Bear with me, honey. It's a tad difficult. . . . Anyway, there was a woman I knew a few years back — stubborn about the whole business of promises. Fine woman, but never *could* get around her when it came to promises. Her name —" He hesitated, shot a sideways glance at Lauren. "Her name was Eleanor Edwards."

Lauren sat frozen, unable to speak or move. Eleanor Edwards. Auntie Nell.

"Years ago I learned she had something I

wanted so badly, I would have moved heaven and earth to get it — but I couldn't move your Auntie Nell. She had you. And she'd made a promise."

A suspicion was growing in Lauren's mind — a possibility that she couldn't quite believe. She looked at Perry, who sat very still, his eyes full of unasked questions, and then at the old man beside her. "Pops?" she asked softly. She couldn't say anymore.

"I had a son," Pops said. "He was in the Navy, stationed in San Francisco. Matt was a fine boy." Pops seemed to be looking sadly into a far distance, seeing another world and another time.

"He wrote home that he'd found a wonderful girl. Said he was in love. Said he'd bring her back with him. His mother and I — Well, we were happy for him, and we hoped it would all work out. We were a little worried — he was happy-go-lucky and impetuous. . . ."

Lauren said nothing but put her hand on Pops's arm. He gave her a faint smile. "Then he didn't say any more about her. And when he came home at last, he wasn't the same boy. He wasn't a boy at all, not anymore. He was a man, an unhappy man who wouldn't talk about the time he spent in San Francisco."

"My . . . father?" She could hardly get the words out.

Pops nodded slowly. "Three years after he got home, he was diagnosed as having leukemia. Finally, when he knew the doctors couldn't do any more for him, he told me the story.

"Your mama knew she was pregnant, honey, but she didn't want to get married. Didn't want to move back to the Midwest, she said, and be a suburban housewife with things like PTA and car pools. Matt couldn't change her mind, though God knows he tried. He died not knowing whether his baby had been a boy or a girl. But I couldn't leave it like that, could I?"

Of course he couldn't. Not Pops. Perry was leaning forward now, intent, and Lauren felt tears brim in her eyes and spill over. Her throat was so tight, she couldn't speak.

"Well." Pops looked down at his hands. "I hired a private detective. Took us forever. Mary — your grandmother — died before we learned all the facts. You were already nine years old. Your mother had died. And you were being guarded ferociously by this stubborn mama dragon you called Auntie Nell. She'd promised your mother she'd never let Matt or his family know where you were, and, by golly, she wasn't about to break her promises."

She found her voice at last. "You're the one

who sent the money, then," she said raggedly. "But why haven't you told me all this before? Why —"

"Hold on, child, I'm not through with this yet. She grudgingly agreed to let me help educate you. Actually, when I finally got out here — I was at your high-school graduation, honey — we got along pretty well, your Auntie Nell and I. And when you reached twenty-one, I said it was time to let you make your own decisions on this whole thing, but Auntie Nell said no. She said she'd promised your mother on her deathbed —" He shook his head. "Never met such a bullheaded woman."

Lauren nodded. Yes, Auntie Nell could be extremely strong minded. Her fingers tightened on Pops's arm.

"But then when she found out how sick she was — Well, she couldn't see leaving you all alone, self-sufficient though you were, and she knew you were unhappy and restless and needed change. So we started making arrangements to get you interested in starting an antiques shop somewhere in my immediate vicinity — which was right here. And here you are."

"Oh, Pops!" The tears were running unchecked now. This was almost too much to take in at one time. She had an almost uncontrollable desire to laugh right through them, but in that direction surely lay a full-blown case of hysterics. "But, Pops, that still doesn't answer the question of why you didn't tell me before," she finally managed, a little accusingly. "Why make such a big secret of it once the decision had been made?"

"Well, darn it, honey, I didn't know whether you'd even *like* me or not, did I? Or even how I'd feel about you once I'd gotten to know you. I just thought I'd give it a little time, not spring it on you all unsuspecting. Figured I'd let you get settled here first. Sometimes, though," he said, his eyes growing wistful, "you smile just the way Matt did. And I think, my goodness, I've got me a granddaughter. And if I live long enough, maybe I'll even have a great-grandchild or two. If certain people just don't put it all off too long, that is."

Perry spoke for the first time since Pops had started his story. "Certain people," he said in judicially measured tones, "would be, I'm sure, very happy to oblige in a joint venture in that particular category."

Lauren looked at him quickly, saw the laughter in his eyes, and brushed away the rest of the dampness on her cheeks with an impatient hand. Out in the yard, a late-foraging robin winged its way gracefully homeward to its nest.

"I'll drink to that," she said, "as soon as you two quit talking long enough to let me go in and get the zinfandel." She rose, planted a kiss on the top of Pops's head, and then for good measure planted one on the top of Perry's. Then, happiness bubbling within her, she repeated the process — and knew that the whole procedure was bringing those joyfully illogical tears back to a threatened flood stage.

So, with some difficulty, she managed to beam tremulously at her two favorite men before she turned to disappear into the dusk of the house with a graceful swirl of ice-blue caftan, carrying with her the knowledge that she was truly home at last.

The employees of THORNDIKE PRESS hope you have enjoyed this Large Print book. All our Large Print titles are designed for easy reading, and all our books are made to last. Other Thorndike Large Print books are available at your library, through selected bookstores, or directly from us. For more information about current and upcoming titles, please call or mail your name and address to:

THORNDIKE PRESS
PO Box 159
Thorndike, Maine 04986
800/223-6121
207/948-2962